An Incommunicado Mountie

Adventures of the First Woman Mountie. Book 11

LAURIE SCHRAMM

Print ISBN: 978-1-7387599-4-1
ePub ISBN: 978-1-7387599-5-8

Laurie Schramm

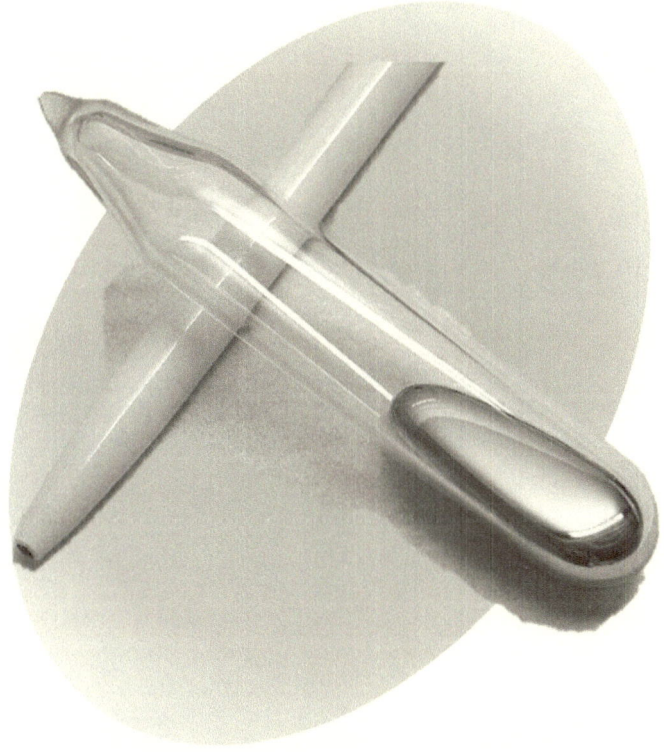

Laurie Schramm

DEDICATION

To Dr. Jim Holmes (Carleton University) and Dr. Ken Hayes (Dalhousie University) for their valuable lessons about the properties and hazards of metal mercury.

Laurie Schramm

CONTENTS

Laurie Schramm

ACKNOWLEDGMENTS

I am extremely grateful to the growing number of friendly readers that that have provided encouragement, comments, and suggestions based on drafts of these books: Ann Marie, Katherine, Victoria, William, Dawson, Al, Jayme, Karen M., and Ernie.

Special thanks also to five real-life veterans of the RCMP, all of whom have supplemented their encouragement with background, advice, and factual reference materials on the Force: Chief Superintendent William Schramm (Ret.), who also kindly allowed my main character to borrow his Regimental Number, Assistant Commissioner Dawson Hovey (Ret.), Deputy Commissioner Peter German, KC, Ph.D. (Ret.), Constable Karen Frost (Ret., one of the trailblazing women Mounties who joined-up when women represented only 2% of the total uniformed complement), and especially Staff Sergeant Al Lund (Ret., author of *Mounties on the Cover* and probably the world's leading authority on Mountie fiction).

Laurie Schramm

LIST OF CHARACTERS
(IN ORDER OF APPEARANCE)

- Corporal Alexandra (Alex) Houston, RCMP Security Service
- Silver, an Alaskan Malamute; and Alex's friend and police-service-dog partner
- Captain Donald (Don) Harrison, Military Intelligence, Canadian Armed Forces
- Patricia (Pat) Lansing, Petroleum Geology student, University of Alberta (U of A)
- Gerry Gilbert, Physics student, U of A
- Merlin, a white and grey Maine Shag cat
- Sandra Hayward, Psychology student, U of A
- Barry Hawkins, Ph.D. student (Chemistry), U of A
- Dr. Dianne Hayward, Medical resident, U of A Hospital
- Gary Parks, M.Eng. student (Mineral Engineering), U of A
- Kate Morrison, Dentistry student, U of A
- Marcel Gerrard, Manager, Pilot Mountain Ski Resort
- Kevin Beach, Lift attendant, Pilot Mountain Ski Resort
- Renée, Housekeeper, Pilot Mountain Ski Resort
- George, General Maintenance and Repair 'Handyman', Pilot Mountain Ski Resort

Laurie Schramm

1 PRELUDE

August, 1978
Edmonton, Alberta

The university campus and its attached teaching hospital were quiet. The summer term had ended and it would be a few weeks before a horde of new and returning students would arrive for the fall term. The campus was especially quiet because it was 6 am on a Sunday morning.

The morning sun was just dawning and, although the parking lots were virtually empty, most of the large buildings still had their interior lights on.

A solitary figure crossed the campus without hesitation. They knew this route well enough to be able to follow it blindfolded. The familiar route led to a very familiar building, and the figure walked up to and through the front door with an air of casual assurance.

Climbing the broad, stone stairs, the figure went up to the third floor and then passed through one of two sets of large double doors. A broad hallway ran the length of the building, half on each side of the staircase. Without hesitation, the figure turned right and headed for one of the many laboratories on this floor – in this case, one of the last two at the end of the hall.

Along the way, occasional glances into some of the many open laboratory doors showed that there were a few people working in some of the labs, even at such an early weekend hour. These were graduate

1

students, *working on their M.Sc. or Ph.D. thesis projects, and/or post-doctoral ('post-doc') research associates, working on team-based research projects. They all looked alike, clothed as they were in faded jeans, white lab coats, and unfashionable safety glasses. Their only distinguishing features were the hair on the backs of their heads: short, long, pony-tailed… one even sported a rather wild-looking 'afro.'*

Whether any of these people heard the figure's quiet footsteps in the hallway was impossible to detect, as not a single one looked up from their work. This, as the figure well knew, was quite normal, making the risk of being observed very low.

The door to the laboratory at the end of the hall was locked, but yielded to one of the keys that the figure produced from a pocket. The figure entered the lab, closed the door, and removed the small daypack they had been wearing. The figure then selected a lab coat from a nearby rack and put it on. In the unlikely event that anyone else came into the lab, it would be important for everything to appear normal; routine even. The lights, like most of the others in the building were already on.

Suitably clothed, the figure made for the back of the lab where a tall, double-doored chemical cabinet stood next to two fume hoods[1]. Selecting another, smaller key from a pocket, the figure unlocked the cabinet doors and swung them open. Before removing anything, however, the figure went to one of the fume hoods. The big glass sliding door was already partly open, and the figure raised it completely open then reached in and switched on its interior light and exhaust fan.

Next, the figure went to one of the three big lab benches that stretched the full length of the laboratory and occupied most of the floor space. The figure walked to exactly the right spot, opened exactly the right drawer, and withdrew a modest-size cardboard case containing ten Pyrex™-glass media bottles of the type that had drip-free pouring rings, and liner-less, plug-seal type leak-proof screw caps. At 25 mL (0.84 oz) each, the bottles weren't particularly large; they didn't need to be. And there was no need to clean them, as they were brand new. Returning to the fume hood, the figure opened the case, withdrew the media vials, unscrewed the caps and placed the bottles in a neat row, with their caps placed to one side. With these preliminaries accomplished, the figure took a wooden step-stool from one corner of the lab, moved it in front of the chemical storage cabinet and stepped up onto the higher of its two steps.

In future years, there would come into place university regulations prohibiting the storage above shoulder height of dangerous chemicals in heavy containers, but it was still only 1979, and people still had a marked tendency to place seldom-used chemicals in the back corners of high shelves. This was a direct consequence of people's natural desire to store the most frequently used chemicals in the most easy-to-reach places.

In the present case, however, the figure was after a chemical that, in this particular laboratory at least, was very rarely used. An advantage of this feature, was that if some of the chemical went missing its loss might not be discovered for years, if ever.

Standing on the top step of the stool, the figure began moving bottles of chemicals away from the front-left side of the top shelf. There were a lot of them, in various sizes and shapes, some made of clear glass, some polypropylene, and others – those that contained chemicals that were prone to degrade in the presence of light – made of amber glass. Eventually, this activity exposed a large, wide-mouth bottle made of heavy, clear glass that was standing in the extreme back, left-hand corner.

That was the one.

Whereas the previous bottles had been moved away one-handed and rather quickly, the figure's manner now changed completely into one of extreme care. Using both hands, the big glass bottle was slid forward on the shelf, then lifted up, off, and down.

It was heavy!

Taking a moment to reset their grip, the figure carefully stepped backwards and down the two steps of the stool, then over to the fume hood. The main working surface of the fume hood was like a mini-lab bench, covered in black, chemical-resistant epoxy and set at a convenient working height for most people. The heavy glass bottle was placed onto this surface, well inside the hood, after which the front glass door was lowered about three-quarters of the way; open enough to permit the figure's hands and forearms to work inside, and closed enough to ensure most fumes remained inside the hood, where they could be sucked away by the exhaust fan.

Now that everything was assembled and ready, the figure opened the top of the big glass bottle and, again holding it with both hands, carefully poured some of its contents into each of the smaller bottles. This particular chemical flowed very easily and smoothly, so it was just a question of having steady hands and proceeding slowly. After each vial had successfully been filled about three-quarters full, the figure replaced the top on the big glass bottle. Next, the caps were carefully screwed onto the smaller bottles, all of which were placed – standing upright - in their original carboard case. Then, the figure raised the sliding glass door of the fume hood completely open.

Done, *the figure thought.*

Remembering in time that this was not the right time to relax, the figure took up the big glass bottle, walked back to the step-stool, stepped up, and then replaced the bottle in the back-left corner of the top shelf with as much care as had been used during its removal in the first place. Next the various bottles that had previously resided in front of the big glass bottle were moved back to their original positions, or at least as nearly to their original positions as the figure could remember. Given that when these latter were originally moved, the figure had taken care to temporarily arrange them in rows that matched their original ordering, then reversed the process when replacing them, every one of them ended up back in almost exactly its original location. With this done, the figure got down, replaced the step-stool in its original position, then closed and locked the doors of the chemical cabinet.

Returning to the fume hood, the figure picked up the case of bottles, switched off the light and exhaust fan in the fume hood, then partially closed its door in an approximation of its original position.

The figure walked to the door of the lab and looked out the small window that is characteristic of all chemical-laboratory doors. The hallway appeared to be deserted.

So far, so good, *the figure thought.*

The figure removed their lab coat and restored it to its former place on the rack, stooped down to place the case containing the glass bottles into the daypack that had been left there on the floor, then rose and partially donned the daypack (meaning that it was worn using only one of its shoulder straps in the prevailing fashion of the day).

The figure paused and took a long, last look around. Everything looked normal. Leaving the lights on, the figure went out, closed the lab door, and relocked it.

Finally, the figure strolled down the hallway, down the main stairway, and out of the building as if it were the sort of thing that they had done a thousand times before.

This, with the exception of the theft of the chemical, was the absolute truth.

2 ALPINE MEADOWS

Day 1: Friday, October 19, 1979
Banff National Park, Alberta

Vacation time, at last, I thought to myself as Don and Silver and I drove north along the Trans-Canada Highway to a new ski resort that was opening high up in the Rocky Mountains.

My name is Corporal Alexandra Houston, Royal Canadian Mounted Police (RCMP) Security Service. Yes, I'm a woman Mountie. My friends call me Alex. Silver, an Alaskan Malamute, is a Police Service Dog (PSD) and my friend and partner. Don is Captain Don Harrison, Royal Canadian Air Force (RCAF), working in Military Intelligence. He is also my fiancé.

This was actually a second attempt at a vacation for us as, shortly after becoming engaged, Don and I had been invited to a gathering of his family ('the clan') for his grandmother's funeral in Cape Breton, Nova Scotia. Unfortunately, both the family reunion and any hopes for a vacation were hampered by a series of suspicious incidents and a murder[2]. Not the stuff of which relaxing, let alone romantic, vacations are made.

Luckily for us, our respective bosses were sympathetic, and after six months of being back at work in our respective jobs, we were now making a second attempt at a relaxing getaway.

We were well into the fall season by this time, and already the region's larch trees had changed from green to a beautiful gold and then faded as their needles dropped. As we gained elevation in the mountains, you could clearly see that all the trees except evergreens were dropping their leaves and needles. Fall was preparing to make way for winter. That was fine with us, as we were going for the fresh mountain air and some high-altitude hiking in Banff's sub-arctic alpine meadows.

As we turned off the parkway, a winding road took us along and up one side of a valley until we reached a shining new gondola station. The opportunity that had brought us to this particular place was the opening of the new Pilot Mountain Ski Resort.

Pilot Mountain towers over the Bow River Valley in Banff National Park. It is fairly tall, as the Rocky Mountains go, and offers great views along the valley.

It was late fall and the resort had opened before the actual ski season, partly to get some cash flow while they geared-up their staffing and operations. Another reason was that there was some demand on the part of mountaineering hikers and, presumably, people that just wanted to 'get away from it all' and relax in the peace and fresh air of the mountains.

Don and I qualified on both counts. Although there were also good technical mountain climbs in the area, the resort had several hikes that were rated as 'difficult Alpine scrambles', meaning off-trail routes comprising a mixture of rock and high-altitude snow, with a 'non-technical' summit or viewpoint as their destinations. Although such non-technical summits did not require the use of specialized climbing- or glacier-travel equipment, they were arduous enough, requiring travel through brush and scree, up steep slopes, across streams, and over rock-, boulder-, and/or snow-covered slopes.

Accordingly, Don and I had brought appropriate clothing, sturdy hiking boots, and a certain amount of climbing equipment. The latter included medium-duty climbing rope and several widths and lengths of slings – of the sort that could be used to ascend or descend the odd short but very steep slope, especially if slippery from scree or snow, but not the sort that would be needed for proper climbing and belaying.

Our attire and gear immediately distinguished us from those of our companions in the gondola car we'd boarded for the journey up to the resort's lodge. *Soar through the Rockies in comfort*, read one of the resort's brochures, *as you enjoy a 5 km scenic ride. Our gondola comfortably accommodates 6 people per car.*

They must rate gondola cars they way they do tents, I thought to myself, when I saw the cars up close. You could certainly pack six adults into a car, but I don't think the word comfort would be the one that came to people's minds.

It turned out not to be an issue for us, though. There weren't many people preparing to go up the mountain, and Don, Silver, and I were installed in a car with only two other people, who introduced them selves as Pat and Gerry.

As the gondola car was pulled uphill, we were able to enjoy the silence and look out at the views on each side. It was quiet until we reached the first tower, when the spring–loaded grips that attached our car to the cable bounced and rattled over a long series of little wheels. This was somewhat unnerving at first, but only lasted a short time; afterword everything went quiet again until the next tower was reached. At one point, we went through an intermediate lift station where we were detached from the first cable. We were then pulled through the station on tracks that passed a huge bull-wheel (by which the first cable was returned downhill), then curved so that our car made a left-hand turn, then passed a second bull-wheel. After that, our car was automatically attached to a second cable that took us over more towers as we made our way up the rest of the mountain.

Between the scenery and the various mechanical systems, there was much to incite casual conversations, making it a companionable ride.

I couldn't help noticing that Pat and Gerry's clothing and day-packs were of the sort one would choose for an afternoon in a city park: light jackets that would offer some protection as long as there was no cold, wind, or rain, and light runners[3] that would protect the feet as long as one remained on engineered sidewalks and pathways. Not, in other words, the kind of gear that experienced hikers would ever take on hikes in the mountains, regardless of season or altitude.

I was surprised, therefore, when they told us that they had come for the same kinds of alpine hiking and scrambling that had attracted us. *Good luck to you,* I thought, as I remembered one of the sayings of my old mountaineering instructor: *Without the right training and equipment you'll be fine, as long as nothing bad ever happens.*

During the thirty, or so, minute gondola ride, we learned that Pat and Gerry were university-student-friends (i.e., 'just friends') from Edmonton. And that they would be joined later by five other university friends, all for a week of hiking and relaxing.

Pat was a petroleum-geology student, blonde, slightly less than average height, full-figured and extremely outgoing and pleasant. I was to later discover that she was also incredibly energetic and adventurous. In contrast, Gerry was a physics student, tall and thin, with unremarkable brown hair and eyes, and a somewhat ascetic manner.

Gerry explained that he was working on a new theory related to gas pressures, for which the experimental component involved a lot of work with mercury manometers. I would have liked to have heard more but Pat, who had the more outgoing personality, actually did most of the talking and, in fact, kept our conversation going throughout the entire ride to the lodge. To be fair, she had such an energetic personality that her interesting stories made the trip go by quickly.

When we disembarked from the gondola car at the upper station, we were told that we needn't wait for our luggage. It had previously been checked-in, and a gondola attendant pointed out the special cargo car that had the luggage – it looked a bit like a big metal basket on a fish hook – saying that our luggage would be brought to our rooms for us.

Shouldering our daypacks, it was a short walk uphill to the entrance to the lodge complex. We were quite high up. The lodge complex had been built partly wrapped around the mountainside, at an elevation of 1,920 m (6,300 ft). This was considerably lower that the actual summit of the mountain, which was at 2,935 m (9,629 ft). I guessed that one reason for having the lodge at a lower elevation was that people tend to get some degree of altitude sickness at elevations above about 2,500 m (8,000 ft).

Like many mountain ski-lodges, this one had high, open-beam ceilings, an impressive main reception area, plus separate great rooms, restaurant, bar-lounge, ski shop, guest rooms, an outdoor heated swimming pool and a truly massive hot tub.

When we approached the Front Desk, there seemed to be no one around.

"Try ringing the bell," said Pat.

"I don't see any bell to ring," said Gerry, who had reached the desk first and was looking around. Fortunately, the desk clerk had heard our voices and a young man of university-student age emerged from a back room to greet us.

"Welcome to Pilot Mountain," he said.

"I was looking for a bell to ring," said Gerry, sounding a bit irritated, "but you don't seem to have one."

"Ah, yes. I'm sorry about that. We do have a bell, but Merlin doesn't like the sound of it. He actually used to jump up here and push the bell onto the floor all the time. We got tired of that pretty quickly, of course, and glued it to the countertop, so now he simply curls up around it so no one can see it... Merlin!... Move!" he commanded.

As he did so, what I had mistakenly taken to be one of those huge, round Russian Roller Hats of the sort that movie stars wear in Europe actually moved. Fascinated, I watched closely as the 'hat' slowly stood up and straightened out into a long arching stretch that revealed a huge white and grey cat. Sure enough, sitting there on the counter-top was revealed a standard chrome push-bell of the sort you see in hotels all over the world.

"Whoa!" said Don, impressed. "Now that is a cat!"

"What kind of cat is it?" asked Pat excitedly. "I didn't think cats could get that big, except for lions and tigers of course."

"Merlin is a Maine Shag," replied the clerk. "He's a white and grey version of what people call a Maine Coon cat. Some people say they are a cross between a raccoon and a cat, while others say that the name comes from the tabby coat with the raccoon-like tail that many of them have, but the truth is that they're just an interesting breed of cat that originated in Maine in the 18[4] or 19th century[4]. The ones that don't have the raccoon-tail look are usually called Maine Shags."

"How big is he?" asked Gerry, who was getting more interested now.

"He's three feet long if you stretch him out, and he weighs over 20 pounds. The world-record largest cat is a Maine Coon cat that was over four feet long, I looked it up."

As the desk clerk was explaining all this, I instinctively looked over at Silver, who had followed us in, expecting to hear him growl at the huge cat. But I was wrong. He just stood there staring at the cat, as if wondering what it was.

Not surprisingly, Merlin had immediately noticed Silver and was staring at him as well.

"It looks like these two aren't going to get along," offered Gerry, having seen my glance.

"I'm not so sure," I said, slowly, "it seems more like they're trying to figure each other out. It'll be interesting to see what develops."

Returning to business, the desk clerk explained that everything was open, even the ski shop and the larger ski lifts. This despite that fact that they were still working to get everything ready for the ski season, which was likely to open in about a month's time. Depending on when the snow arrived, of course.

Connected to one side of the main building, the resort also featured a series of what they called 'family units', comprising pairs of rooms between which were sandwiched separate living rooms, each of which featured comfortable chairs and couches and a large fireplace. These three-room suites had connecting doors and rather than being rectangular, were slightly wedge-shaped so that in aggregate they partially wrapped around the side of the mountain. All of these particular rooms had sliding glass exterior doors that offered fantastic views of the ski/hiking slopes, the chair lifts, various other mountains in the distance and, of course, the valley down below.

Don and I had booked one of these family suites. As we opened the first door, Silver dove in to run from room to room, sniffing and exploring everything. "This is going to be great!" I said to Don, having taken a look at the fireplace room and the views from the big glass doors.

Knowing that Silver – who is a big dog - insisted on sleeping curled up with me, Don selected the bedroom that had two queen-sized beds, leaving me to take the one with the king.

"What'll we do when we're married?" asked Don.

"Something tells me that we're going to have a big furry comforter in between us," I said.

"Hmm, with cold paws too, I'll bet".

"Don't forget the wet nose, and a long, slobbery tongue," I added, but I wasn't worried, knowing that Don had become almost as close to Silver as I was. Besides, although Silver liked to cuddle up with me at night, I'd learned that it only lasted until he was sure that I'd fallen asleep and wouldn't be leaving him. After that, he'd go find his own corner before falling into deeper- and REM-sleep[5].

We still had most of the afternoon left and were eager to get outside, so we decided to explore the area around the lodge first. There was a bunny hill[6] right beside the lodge, with a rope-tow installed, but not operating of course. Further afield, there were three visible lifts: a T-bar[7] and two chair lifts. The T-bar lift wasn't operating either, naturally, but the two chair lifts were operating, so we headed for the one that would take us the highest.

As we walked, we encountered a young couple – in their early twenties perhaps - that seemed to be heading in the same direction.

"Can we say hello to your dog?" the man asked.

"Sure, just start by slowly putting your hand out so he can sniff you... His name's Silver."

As the man did so, he seemed so relaxed and friendly that I was pretty sure Silver would be fine. Sure enough, after a lengthy series of sniffs and a small lick for taste, Silver gave him a friendly look in return and accepted an ear rub.

"My name's Barry. This is Sandra," said the young man.

Silver seemed rather pointedly unimpressed with Barry, but he clearly took an instinctive liking to Sandra, as he immediately walked over to her and rubbed his body along her leg, in the same manner as a cat seeking some petting.

"He likes you already," I said to Sandra as she bent over to give him an ear rub. "He almost never does that with a stranger."

It seemed to make Sandra glow, and Don and I introduced ourselves while she continued petting Silver.

There were so few other people around that it was natural for us all to walk together and chat. Barry was of medium height and build, and seemed to be naturally outgoing and friendly. Sandra, in contrast, was quite petite and reserved to the point of seeming timid. The latter impression was reinforced by her tendency to cling to Barry as we walked.

We quickly learned that they would be staying at the lodge for a short holiday, just like we were, and that they were both university students. Sandra was studying psychology and Barry was studying chemistry. When we mentioned that we'd met two other students coming up on the gondola, Sandra asked about them and quickly confirmed that they were friends of theirs "from U of A," meaning the University of Alberta.

I mentioned that I had been a chemistry student myself at one time, which led to a conversation with Barry about where and what I'd studied. I learned that he was a graduate student, studying for his Ph.D., and that he was specializing in physical chemistry. I had specialized in analytical chemistry, then left university after getting my bachelor's degree, but had learned enough to be able to understand the surface chemistry problem he was studying and the experimental methods he was using, if not the detailed theory behind it all. As a result, we discussed science for a while as we walked.

Meanwhile, being somewhat left out, Don struck up a conversation of some sort with Sandra who seemed willing enough but spoke in a quiet voice.

Between the scenery, weather, and companionable conversations we had a nice walk and time passed so quickly that we soon found ourselves at one of the chair lifts. The particular lift we'd selected was a high-speed quad, meaning that each chair could hold four-people and carry them uphill with a rope speed of about 5 m/s (just over 16 ft/s), making the whole thing quite impressive looking.

Almost immediately, Sandra seemed to have second thoughts about getting on. With much encouragement from Barry, she agreed to give it a try, but she was clearly nervous about it. Her anxiety only increased when she had trouble getting herself onto the chair when their turn came. Although the operator slows the pace of the chairs at the boarding point, it still takes a bit of reflex and coordination to get up onto the chairs, and Sandra had so much trouble that she was right on the edge of falling off the boarding platform when Barry interceded at the last second to pick her up bodily, place her on the chair, and then hop on himself just in the nick of time.

As the chair lifted up, and Barry brought the safety bar down in front of them, I overheard the lift operator give out a relieved sigh and then had to focus on boarding myself. I'd been on chair lifts before, so that I knew what to do, but I wasn't sure what Silver would think about it all. I needn't have worried, however. After I'd gone on and settled myself first, he happily jumped up to sit on the seat beside me, and then shifted to make room as Don got on, and we were off.

The views were already much better from the vantage point of our chair as it was pulled up a long, steep incline, and we had lots of time to look at the resort area below us, and the mountains and valley extending to our left and to our right. I was interested to see that Silver's interest was mostly focused on the various people down below us, and the occasional dog, of course.

When we reached the last of the chair-lift's towers, Silver simply leapt off, leaving Don and I to slip off and follow.

"Well, that was easy," remarked Don. "He's certainly been adaptable."

"Amazingly so," I agreed. "Look at all the places we've been and things we've done, and nothing seems to phase him."

"*Grruph*," said Silver, doing his best to listen to us, as always, while leaning into my hand as I gave him an ear rub.

Sandra and Barry had already gone off on their own, so from the lift station we just walked around enjoying the alpine meadow, which in this case comprised alternating patches of short grass and exposed rock. Had we been there in the spring, the grassy areas would have been full of beautifully-coloured flowering plants. At this time of year, however, the flowers were gone, leaving the scenic vistas as the main attraction.

For me, views were rivalled by two other things: the silence and the fresh mountain air. Just as ocean air has its own particular scent and feel, so does the high-altitude air in the mountains. In the latter case it is partly that it's dry, cool, and clean-smelling, but I've always sensed – or imagined – a special kind of taste to it as well. As a result, I was more than content to just stand and take it all in for a while. The temperature was nice too, at +3°C (37°F). This was much cooler than way down below at the base of the mountain, of course, but still very pleasant since we were dressed for it. It was all very refreshing, and relaxing.

We spent some more time strolling around the meadows. The chair lift had brought us to an elevation of 2,440 m (8000 ft). This point was above the tree-line[8], but still in the 'shadow' of the summit of Pilot Mountain, which projected an additional 500 m above us. We planned to try scrambling to the summit itself after taking a day or two to rest and get our bearings.

When it was time to descend, and we were approaching the chair lift, we again saw Sandra and Barry trying to get onto a chair. This time Barry had boarded first and was trying to help Sandra by pulling her up onto the seat beside him. That should have worked, although Sandra didn't seem to be able to board on her own, and her movements seemed to be almost exactly the wrong ones for enabling Barry to help her. In the end, they managed to get her facing the right direction and her bottom onto the seat, but with her arms and legs sticking out in all different directions, just before the chair lifted up and off the platform.

As they settled themselves and the safety bar came down in front of them, I released the breath I hadn't realized I'd been holding the whole time. "Whew," I said.

"Whew is right," agreed Don. "A few more trips like that and she'll either get the hang of it and laugh it off, or never want to come to a ski hill again."

It would have been quite comical except that Don and I were well aware of the potential for injury.

When we arrived at the lift station ourselves, we got to do something that skiers rarely do: take the chair-lift downhill. This was something I'd never done before and, as you might expect, it was even better going down because the full expanse of mountain and valley views lie open before us the whole way. Fantastic!

During our afternoon hiking around, we'd passed a number of other people, ranging from individuals, two pairs and couples, to slightly larger groups, a few of these having a dog with them like we did. Other than smiling and nodding, and exchanging a few pleasantries (Canadians love to talk about the weather!), we didn't really get introduced to any of them – except for Sandra and Barry of course.

We did meet some more at supper, however.

Silver wasn't allowed in the dining room, of course, but we thought we'd have supper there anyway, since it was our first night. It was in the dining room that we discovered how few people were actually staying at the lodge overnight. In the afternoon, we had encountered and/or seen quite a few people roaming around the meadows near the lodge. Now, in contrast, there only seemed to be ourselves plus seven others. The latter were seated at two adjoining tables and seemed to already know each other quite well.

We'd already met Pat Lansing and Gerry Gilbert while riding up in the gondola, and then Sandra Hayward and Barry Hawkins on our afternoon strolls. Before leaving the dining room, they brought their other three friends over to meet us.

Pat, who was very outgoing, led off saying "We thought it

would be a good idea to get acquainted since there are so few of us staying up here. It will make things more comfortable; don't you think?"

Don and I agreed and introduced ourselves as an engaged couple on vacation; me from Ottawa and Don from Halifax.

"And they have a big dog that looks like a wolf!" added Pat.

"His name's Silver," I supplied. "He's an Alaskan Malamute and former dog-sled leader."

Pat then proceeded to introduce Dianne Hayward, Gary Parks, and Kate Morrison.

Dianne was of medium height, pretty, Raven-haired, and very slender. She said a few appropriate things but seemed rather aloof in her manner. Gary, in contrast, was big: over six feet tall and heavyset, sporting fashionable hair (meaning thick, long, and a bit wild). He was wearing a lumberjack-style shirt, which we were to discover was a fixture with him, and he certainly looked the part of a stereotypical British Columbian lumberjack. Beyond his sheer size, he almost radiated a sense of strength and solidarity. He didn't say much, but I was most taken by his blue eyes, which had a mischievous-looking sparkle to them, as if he found people and life entertaining.

Kate Morrison was the last to be introduced. She was of medium height and build, with dark brown hair and piercing ice-blue eyes that were very much like Silver's eyes. She didn't say anything when introduced but simply nodded her head in a manner that suggested a haughty arrogance. *Maybe she'll warm up as time goes on*, I thought, in an attempt to be generous.

Pat had introduced Dianne and Gary as a couple, which caused their expressions to change, but I couldn't judge what that might mean. In any case, everyone seemed friendly enough, befitting people on vacation.

Later that evening, Don and I went to try the outdoor hot tub. It was shaped somewhat like a boomerang, presumably to maximize the amount of seating space along the periphery, and it was huge – easily as large as some hotels' swimming pools. The whole thing was enclosed by a low wall of glass panes, leaving a feeling of wide-open outdoor space and, of course, having great views of the surrounding mountains.

Pat and Gerry were already there, when we arrived, and rather than seem unfriendly, we swam over to sit near them. The topics of conversation were of the 'where are you from' and 'what do you do' variety, so we told them the truth, but only parts of the whole truth. I explained that I was a Mountie and that Silver was a police-service dog, but not the part of the Force to which we were assigned nor the type of work we do. For his part, Don explained that he was in the RCAF and elaborated that he was in communications and electronics engineering, but left out his assignment to military intelligence and the many other identities that he assumed from time to time.

It was Don's engineering background that prompted a run-down from Pat on her companions. We already knew that she and Gerry were students in petroleum-geology and physics, respectively. We also knew that Sandra was in psychology and that Barry was a Ph.D. student in chemistry. Pat explained that Dianne was Sandra's sister, and that she - Dianne - was a physician and medical resident at the teaching hospital. Gary, she said, was a Masters student in mineral engineering, while Kate was studying dentistry.

As one thing led to another, Pat also explained some of the dynamics in their little group. "Barry is kind of the centre-piece because, before Sandra, it was he and Dianne that were a couple, and before that it was him and Kate. So now Barry's with Sandra and Dianne's with Gary, and Kate is unattached."

"But everyone still gets along?" asked Don.

"Oh yes, we're all good friends and everyone's left the past in the past and moved on so everything's good," said Pat with a bright, cheery smile.

I was inclined to take her word for it, but the glance Don shot at me suggested that he thought it unlikely. In any case, with these interpersonal preliminaries established, the topics of conversation broadened and diffused, although we mostly just soaked in companionable silence and enjoyed the setting we'd come to.

"Looks like we're in the company of an intelligent and well-educated bunch," I remarked as we walked back to our rooms.

"Yes, but beyond that they're all very different from each other," Don replied.

"Physically, you mean?" I asked.

"Yes, that too, but I was thinking of personalities."

"Mmm. You think a week of semi-isolation up here will bring

out some rough edges?"

"Maybe. For the two couples, it may be a bit of a test. Especially with two of Barry's ex-girlfriends in the gang... I wonder who dumped whom."

"I see where you're heading. Barry reminds me of someone I knew in university that seemed to jump from girlfriend to girlfriend and somehow the ex-girlfriends kept showing up to see him as if they were all trying to get him back. I never really understood the attraction he had for so many girls, nor how he managed to 'love and leave' them without them being turned off by him."

"Interesting. Maybe we'll see some fireworks in a few days," then he seemed to pause in thought. After a moment he continued. "How about us, then?" he asked.

"Are you kidding?" I poked him in the ribs. "After all we've been through together?"

That produced quiet chuckles from both of us.

In hindsight, of course, we shouldn't have been so frivolous in our speculations about the others, but we weren't to know what was coming.

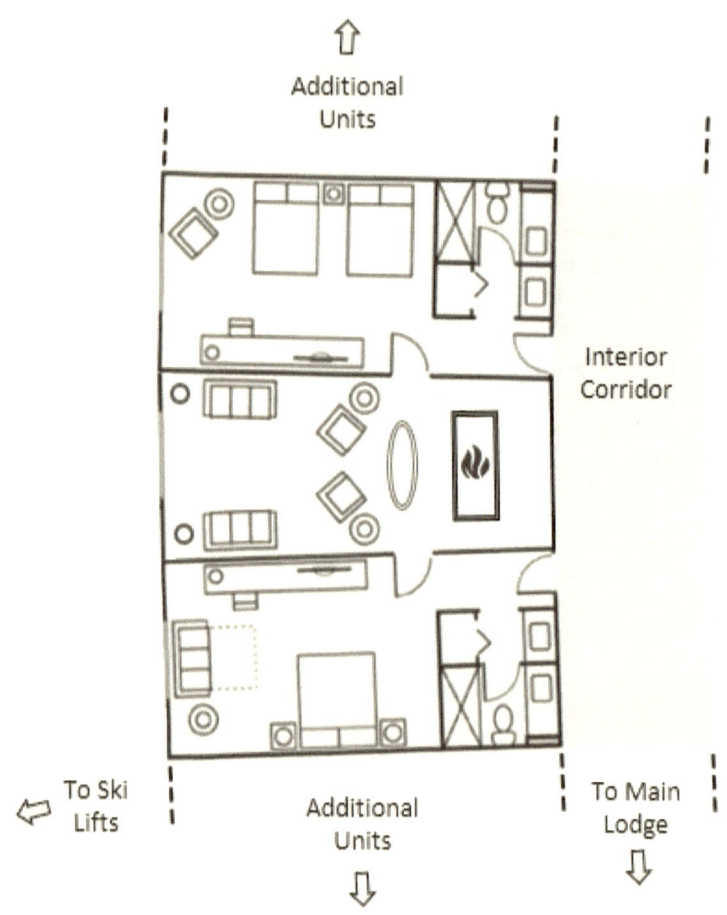

Additional
Units

Interior
Corridor

To Ski
Lifts

Additional
Units

To Main
Lodge

The Mountain-Top Ski Lodge

3 VACATION AT LAST

Day 2: Saturday, October 20, 1979
Pilot Mountain, Banff National Park, Alberta

The first order of business on vacation is usually to get rested which, in this case, involved sleeping in late. By the time I did get up, the mid-morning sun was streaming in through the windows and a quick peek outside confirmed that the sky was clear.

After sending Silver over to Don's room to wake him up, we got dressed for walking around: shorts, light tops, hiking boots, plus fleece sweaters and rain shells in case the weather were to change, which can happen quickly in the mountains. By the time we were dressed, our room-service orders for breakfast had arrived and following breakfast we were ready to walk around some more.

This time we made for the only other chair lift that was operating. Whereas the one we had taken the day before had the most elevation gain, this second one was actually a longer ride as it carried us up and around the side of the mountain, much further away from the lodge. As we approached the lift, we could see that it was another high-speed quad and there were three people boarding just ahead of us. These were Pat, Gerry and Kate, whom we'd met the previous day, and all three were getting onto a single chair.

In contrast to the misadventures of Barry and Sandra the previous afternoon, this trio was either composed of veteran skiers or else they were naturally more agile because the three of them stepped up and slid onto the chair with such fluid ease that it might have been choreographed.

When we reached the lift, I got on first and Silver once again hopped on as if he'd been doing it all his life, followed by Don. This time, the ride on the chair lift was amazing. Whereas the lift we'd taken on the previous day simply took us directly up higher on the mountain, this one traversed a lot of the mountain as it took us diagonally upwards. As a result, as we began our ascent, we had fantastic views of one valley below us that stretched around to the northeast, followed by views of a completely separate valley stretching to the southwest, as we curved around the mountain.

When it was time for us to disembark, Silver leapt off first, followed by Don and I. As we took a few steps away from the lift station then paused to consider which way to go, we found ourselves standing near Pat, Gerry and Kate, all of whom came over to say hi. Pat and Gerry had already met Silver on the gondola ride up the mountain the previous day, but Kate asked if she could meet him.

I was about to give my usual warning about approaching slowly and putting out a hand for him to sniff first, but Kate obviously had experience with animals because she was already doing exactly that, accompanied by a calm, friendly greeting. Silver surprised us both, however, by bracing himself and growling at her. It was a low growl, to be sure, but a growl nonetheless.

I don't know which of us was more surprised, me or Kate, but she pulled back obligingly and I apologized. "I'm sorry Kate, he doesn't usually growl at people. Maybe you have some scent on your clothes that is worrying him."

"Well, I do have two Siamese cats at home, and my clothes are probably full of their scent – and their hair!"

"That could do it all right. Silver is usually a bit wary of cats, but not to the point of chasing them."

"I hear he's a police dog?" she said.

"That was me blabbing," said Pat.

I smiled and said, "That's OK," to Pat and "Yes, he's a police service dog," to Kate, who frowned. "But I thought police dogs were usually German shepherds," she said.

"You're right. Almost all RCMP dogs are German shepherds. There are a few other breeds used for specialty work though. I guess you could say that Silver's one of those."

"There can't be many that look like wolves though, are there?"

"No," I laughed. "Silver is an Alaskan Malamute and he's the only one in the service."

"And you're beautiful, aren't you Silver?" said Kate, who had persisted in her attempts to make friends with Silver. She'd clearly been successful because she was by now briskly rubbing Silver's shoulders and sides, while Silver looked over at me as if to say, "*Well, this is nice!*"

It was surprising to see what a change had come over Kate. When we'd met her the evening before, she'd seemed quite aloof and haughty but animals, or dogs at least, seemed to be a key to softening her manner.

No one explicitly suggested hiking together. It was more that our conversation continued as we started walking such that we found ourselves continuing on together. The three students were good company, and our topics of conversation ranged widely.

Although the views were different, the topography was similar to that of the previous day, with its alternating patches of short grass and exposed rock, and we simply walked around enjoying the alpine meadow. Beyond a few birds flying around, there wasn't much to see in the way of wildlife, which made the other species we did see all the more noticeable.

We heard the marmots before we spotted them. The hoary marmot is a kind of large ground squirrel that inhabits the upper elevations of the Canadian Rocky Mountains, and is noteworthy for its piercing whistle. There are several variations of this whistle, which they use to communicate with each other. We were lucky enough to see a few marmots scurrying around, a couple eating the wild grasses, and one that seemed to be standing up and looking around at the scenery but was obviously serving as a lookout for the rest. I glanced over at Silver more than once, to make sure that he wasn't thinking about chasing them, but he'd never shown much interest in scurrying creatures. At one point, he even gave me a very direct, injured-seeming gaze that seemed to suggest that I needn't worry, because chasing such defenseless little creatures was beneath his dignity.

Our hike wasn't quite above the tree-line this time, but the broad lanes of forest that had been cleared to make the ski runs provided lots of options for roaming around and getting good views of the valleys below.

As we continued to explore, we eventually caught sight of a couple of grouse near a stand of spruce trees. Pat got quite excited about these, saying "They're called Franklin's Grouse. See the white markings on the birds' tails? They are a kind of spruce grouse, and they actually eat the needles that fall from the spruce trees!"

"Ugh! You won't find me trying to eat spruce needles," remarked Kate.

After about an hour of this, we were getting hungry so when we came across a few layers of exposed rocks that made a convenient place to sit, we stopped to eat a late lunch. The lodge had provided box lunches for us and, in addition to the extra water that Don and I carried, I had in my pack some dog food and a collapsible bowl for Silver.

Whereas meeting Silver had caused Kate to warm up, it was altitude and altitude sickness that caused Gerry to open up more. This was triggered by Kate mentioning that she wasn't feeling hungry.

"Is that usual?" asked Gerry, seemingly not realizing that that could be a very personal question for someone.

"No, it's not," said Kate, reflectively. "I also have a headache, and I seem to be getting tired more easily than usual too.

"Ahhh. It's because of the elevation we're at up here," Gerry said. "That, and the fact that we gained the altitude so quickly yesterday. If we'd taken a couple of days and hiked up here, then you wouldn't feel the altitude so much because your body would have been able to acclimatize along the way."

"Maybe, but then I'd be exhausted from all the hiking. I think I'll take the gondola anytime over the hike if you don't mind."

Gerry laughed. "Me too, come to think of it. Anyway, I think your body is simply having trouble getting enough oxygen in. That's why we're all trying to breather faster than normal, even just sitting here."

"I know the theory, thank you, I've just never experienced it before. And I guess I didn't really expect to, coming up here."

"Anyone bring an altimeter with them?" he asked, and looked pleased but surprised when I dug mine out of a small pouch that I had attached to one of the shoulder straps of my daypack. He thanked me when I handed it over, and read the dial.

"Look like we're at about 2,300 metres. That's about 7,500 feet.

The hiking guides will tell you that altitude sickness generally occurs above 2,500 metres – that's about the altitude the other chair lift took us to yesterday – but some people feel it at lower altitudes."

Kate made a face at this, and said "How is it that you don't seem to be minding the altitude?"

I half expected him to make some kind of crack about male superiority or physical conditioning, but I'd under-estimated him.

"No offense," he hurried on. "It's not your fault. It varies with the individual and seems to be wired into our individual genetics. The best thing you can do is not overexercise. Just let us know when you feel like you should go back to the lodge for a rest, and we'll come with you."

"Thanks," she said, gratefully, "but I'm OK for now."

Gerry thanked me as he handed back my altimeter.

"At least there don't seem to be many bugs up here," said Pat, in an attempt to change the topic of conversation. "One reason I like doing geology field trips in the fall is because it avoids the black fly and mosquito seasons."

This triggered a flurry of black fly horror stories and, since everyone seemed to have one, we took turns relating them as we resumed hiking in the meadows. My own story came from a Canada Day (July 1) long-weekend canoe-camping trip in Kejimkujik National Park, in southwestern Nova Scotia. Some days, we'd had to cover everything, including wearing light cotton gloves and Army-surplus head-net hats – the ones with the mosquito netting that comes down over your face and neck. The only way we could even eat was to cook our food, then rush into our tents to eat it where we could take the gloves and hats off. Horrible! Even just writing about it now is making the back of my neck feel itchy. By the way, I'm not recommending this procedure for eating. We had been very fortunate that there weren't bears around on that trip, because our tents and sleeping bags must have been rich with the scents of food.

By late afternoon, Kate was visibly tiring and by unspoken agreement we hiked back to the chair lift and from there back to the lodge.

When we reached the front of the lodge, the big doors were shut and there standing right in front of them was Merlin the cat, looking for all the world like it was about time some human servant came along and opened the doors for him. This was Silver's chance to investigate the cat more closely, and I watched with trepidation as Silver approached him.

As it turned out, my worry was unnecessary, as Silver and Merlin, gave each other another close stare, after which Merlin seemed to relax and stood motionless while Silver gave him a good sniffing from front to back. They made quite a pair. Although Merlin was a huge cat, by cat standards, his 14-inch shoulder height didn't look so large standing there right next to Silver's 30-inch-high shoulders. With his big bushy tail, however, Merlin's body length was almost as long as Silver's.

With the two of them staring straight at me, I didn't have any trouble reading their body language. "I think they want me to open the door for them," I said to Don and the others.

"Like most cats, Merlin probably thinks he owns the place and we humans were put on earth to serve him," quipped Don. "I'm surprised that Silver's taking his side though."

"Yes, there's some kind of connection there, I think," I said as I stepped forward to open one of the big front doors and then took a step back so the animals could go in first, which they did; together; and quite regally, I thought.

At supper, Pat came over to our table to invite Don and I to join the friends later that evening, in the shared living room of Gary and Gerry's family suite, which was right next to ours. It turned out that Dianne and Pat, and Gary and Gerry, respectively, were each sharing the same kind of suites which were located further down the hall, while Kate had a single room - with no view - across the hall.

After dropping in to see them, we hadn't been visiting long before someone suggested playing a board game from the selection made available by the resort. The game chosen was a popular world-domination-type battle game involving a combination of diplomacy – meaning deal-making and breaking – military battles, and chance. The idea of the game is for players to amass troop markers and take turns attempting to invade and conquer more and more territories until they have control of the entire board (which contained a stylized map of the world). To do so required a combination of strategy and luck, as the 'battles' were conducted by throwing dice and an attacking player had to be careful of the risks involved in being too aggressive because any conquered territories had to be defended against subsequent player-attackers.

The game supported up to six players, so there were too many of us, but Don and Gary were more interested in watching the Saturday night Hockey Night in Canada game on the TV. I said that I'd prefer to just watch, so that left six to play the game. I was somewhat surprised that Dianne and Kate agreed to play, given their tendencies to sometimes be fairly aloof and condescending, but they did.

I didn't mind sitting out. I had played the game before, and always found it interesting to see which people were competitive enough to become thoroughly engrossed and lose sight of the fact that it was 'just a game.' Honesty compels me to admit that I'm a borderline case of that myself.

The early stages of the game are somewhat mechanical, as each player effectively has to decide on a continent to begin with and start positioning and amassing troops. After several rounds of this, however, territories become established and the battles become more intense. By mid-way into the game, wins and losses are being experienced by all players and emotions rise. Not long after that, the more engaged players are visibly crowing over their wins, mourning their losses, offering unwanted and self-serving advice to other players and, forming and betraying alliances. It is at this point that the more competitive players generally become extremely noticeable.

That evening's game was no exception. By the time the game was well underway and approaching the point at which some players risked being wiped out completely, I was able to discern each player's risk appetites and risk tolerances.

Sandra played a cautious, defensive game and would generally use her turns to obtain some armies, build defenses, and settle in to try to hold them. Her boyfriend Barry, in contrast, was always willing to take risks, and sometimes large ones, all the while becoming increasingly impatient and emotional. As the game flow ebbed one way and then another, he was quick to anger when he lost and quick to cool off and gloat when he won.

Dianne played a cool, detached kind of game in which she only took moderate risks and progressed very methodically. Occasionally however, when an opportunity arose, she would pounce on it with everything she had no matter the risk. This made her a difficult player to predict.

Of the Pat and Gerry couple, Pat played a *Blitzkrieg* style, in that she would advance as fast as she could, often to the very limit of her available forces, taking her chances with the dice and hoping that conquering a large number of countries would offset their minimal or nonexistent defenses. Gerry was just as risk tolerant as Pat, but I eventually discerned that he had a strategy right from the beginning of the game, and he stuck to it like glue. As a result, his moves were patient and methodical, and only the fortunes of the dice rolls affected his ability to advance or not on each turn.

Kate's style was different again. She was a moderate risk taker, had no apparent strategy, and simply went with opportunities as they arose. This led to her having small pockets of success, but never in a way that enabled her to conquer entire continents and establish solid defenses.

Gerry's the one to beat, I thought, *unless pure chance favours the high-risk gambles of Barry or Dianne.*

Another interesting dynamic that was being played out during the game was interpersonal. It had quickly become obvious that Sandra and Barry were effectively playing as a couple, in that Sandra would never attack Barry and Barry would seldom attack her, except when necessity forced him to cross one of her territories in order to get at someone else. This meant that Barry could afford to leave any borders with Sandra undefended, a fact that caused considerable dismay among the other players, whose whispering and arguing made it clear that they understandably considered this to be an unfair advantage.

Meanwhile, although nothing was ever said out loud about it, Dianne and Kate seemed to take a special delight in attacking Sandra at every opportunity. It was only a game, of course, but the fact that both women were former girlfriends of Barry made me wonder how amicable their separations had been. If so, Barry seemed oblivious to any such nuances and continued attacking everyone but Sandra with a reckless abandon that succeeded more often than not.

At the halfway point Gary was ahead, with Gerry running a close second, but then the dynamics changed. Recognizing that she was in danger of losing the game, Dianne dropped any pretense to pleasantries or sense of humour, and began changing strategies. For a while, this worked, and her troops advanced, overtaking the markers of less strategic - or simply unlucky - players. A combination of strategy, luck, and a continual series of alliances that were betrayed as quickly as they were made, enabled her to become the player with the strongest position.

After an hour and a half of play, Sandra, Pat, and Kate had all been wiped out and the game was down to Dianne, Barry and Gerry. At this point, Dianne was no longer able to make alliances and her momentum slowed. As it did, a fierce determination to destroy Barry seemed to emerge as she began to attack him at times when she really should have been more worried about Gerry. This reinforced my suspicion that there might be a hidden, unresolved interpersonal issue lying there. In fact, if it hadn't been for Dianne, Barry might have won.

But it was Gerry, with his careful but relentless advances that ultimately prevailed. Gerry was humble and gracious in his win, but I could tell that he was pleased.

Barry, meanwhile, had purposely tipped the board game over – sending the markers flying all over the place – then got up and stormed out, all the while swearing and cursing the world in general. We could still hear him cursing as he stamped down the hallway.

Dianne, for her part, arose from the game with a tight smile of satisfaction, announced herself tired and went off to bed, leaving the remaining players to lick their wounds.

Sandra and Kate disappeared shortly thereafter, neither having done much beyond scowl after the close of the game. As the door closed behind them, Pat's cheerful voice broke the spell.

"Don't mind them," she advised. "They do this all the time, no matter what the game is. Barry and Dianne are so competitive that it's a wonder they have any friends, especially Gerry and Gary," she added, pointedly looking over toward the TV where Gary and Don were still engrossed in the hockey game.

That seemed like a cue, so I ventured a question that was really none of my business. "Is there some other issue between Dianne and Barry...? I mean, the attacking seemed almost personal after a while."

Pat looked thoughtfully at me for a moment, then said "I can see why you're a policewoman. I bet you don't miss much... Yes, I think I already told you that Dianne and Barry used to be a couple, but there's more to it than that. Over time, Barry's affections shifted more towards her sister until eventually Barry and Dianne broke up. I have to admit that it's also crossed my mind that Dianne may have taken up with Gary in hopes of creating jealousy on Barry's part."

"And they'll all be friends again tomorrow morning?" I couldn't help asking.

Pat giggled. "I wouldn't go that far. Don't be surprised if things feel a bit chilly at breakfast, but they'll warm up as the day goes on… They always do."

Gary, I noticed, hadn't said a word during this discussion, but I could see in his eyes that he'd paid attention and had had heard everything. Apparently, he just didn't have anything he felt like contributing to the conversation.

"An interesting collection of personalities," said Don later, as we walked back to our own rooms.

"Yes. Tomorrow should be interesting."

Merlin

Laurie Schramm

4 A MOUNTAIN SCRAMBLE

Day 3: Sunday, October 21, 1979
Pilot Mountain, Banff National Park, Alberta

At breakfast the next morning, Pat's prediction was borne out.

Don and I were sitting together at our own table and, I have to admit, we were quite enjoying ourselves.

It was different, of course, for the group of seven friends who were once again arranged around two tables for four that had been pulled together. From our vantage point, we had no trouble observing that Pat, Gary, Kate, and even Gerry, made considerable efforts at small talk but without much success. Dianne was occasionally drawn into the discussions, but otherwise remained largely aloof. Barry, however, maintained a grumpy expression and injured silence. This, apparently, was a legacy of the result of previous evening's board game and whatever other bad feelings might lie below the surface as a result of his feelings about the other players' conduct.

After breakfast, Don and I went to assemble our gear for the day.

The first serious hike we had planned was to go up Pilot Mountain itself, the summit of which towered over the entire ski area and is one of the most visible mountains to drivers of the Trans-Canada Highway as it follows the Bow Valley. According to our hiking guidebook, Pilot Mountain got its name (in 1884) because it was a key landmark for 19th-century travellers in the region.

Although it was an uphill hike/scramble all the way, the first part comprised easy hiking through forests of spruce, fir, and the occasional alpine larch. Here, the paths were covered in thick moss, which made them look like something out of a fairy-tale. Between our elevation and the surrounding forest, it was quiet; beautifully quiet.

This is what we came for, I thought to myself.

For the second part of the route, we followed an animal trail that ran beside what in the summer and fall was a drainage path, but which in the winter and spring was an avalanche chute. This was easy to follow, because the spring avalanches kept the trees well cleared.

We didn't run into any animals on the trail besides an occasional grouse that would skitter a bit and then run to hide on one side. We did lose the trail a few times due to the presence of rock slides, but by following the drainage chute we were always able to find it again. Scrambling over the rock slides was much more difficult for Silver than for Don and I, and I was grateful for the excuse to slow down a bit.

After skirting around a rock wall, our terrain began the transition from mostly forest to alpine tundra and we began to emerge from the tree-line[8]. As we did so, we were presented with more and more glimpses of the route ahead and of the vistas around us, until finally we were clear of the highest surviving trees, which presented us with a bleak picture of what it took to survive at that altitude. These highest-elevation trees were short, and had become bent and twisted in their continual fight against the wind and cold, but they had survived.

The tree line where we were climbing was at about 2,300 m (7,500 ft) and our hiking guidebook explained that, in the Rocky Mountains, the average rate of decrease in air temperature with increasing altitude was about 1.9 °C (3.5 °F) per 300 m (1,000 ft) of elevation gain. That meant that the temperature was routinely more than 5 °C colder where we were than down by the highway below (which was at an elevation of about 1,450 m). The temperatures at the summit would be another 5 °C colder yet. It is these differences that are responsible for the alpine climate. While a difference of five to ten degrees may not sound like much for the summer, it was clearly the difference between life and death for flora and fauna in the winter.

For the next portion of our route, mostly hiking gave way to mostly scrambling as it was all rock and scree to the summit. In several places we marked our trail with pieces of brightly-coloured flagging so that we would be able to find our way back to the same drainage chute when we returned from the summit.

I said we were scrambling, but we did encounter rock walls along the way. These tended to have layers upon layers of shallow ledges so Don and I could climb them using the toes and sides of our boots to do the work, and our hands and fingers to keep us on balance. My first thought, was that we'd have to abandon further uphill scrambling because of Silver, but I was wrong.

Since the ledges tended to be spaced anywhere from six to ten inches apart, he was able to cross from one side of a wall to the other making small elevation gains along the way, then turn around and come back doing the same thing, effectively making a large number of very shallow switchbacks. It was impressive to see, and it got him to the top of the first rock wall in about the same amount of time it took Don and I. We successfully navigated two large rock walls in this manner, and were very pleased with ourselves although I knew full well that there were many other mountains on which Silver's technique would not work.

After the rock walls, the terrain changed again and we traversed several rock and scree slopes that were quite straightforward. Straightforward except for the need to remain vigilant, because Pilot Mountain is made up of sedimentary rock from ancient, shallow seas. The practical importance of the mountain's geology is that the upper slopes have so much loose, broken, and layered rock that can give way without warning, sending a hiker sliding – or tumbling - a long way down the mountain.

After that, there was a longish haul along a ridge on one shoulder of the mountain and then the summit itself, which was simply a cap made of more broken rock.

The first time I'd ever climbed a mountain, I'd expected some kind of exhilaration and emotional climax, and had been somewhat disappointed to feel mostly just tired. But, as has been said before by many others, and in many different contexts: 'it's the journey not the destination' that brings both the challenges and the satisfactions. According to our hiking guidebook, the first ascent of Pilot Mountain was in 1885, by a geological survey team, and it felt somehow historically significant to have climbed it ourselves, nearly a hundred years later.

We did, of course, enjoy the 360° views. We had a great view of the closest mountain: Copper Mountain. With the aid of our 'topo' (topographic) map, we were able to identify several other mountains, including two that formed part of the Massive Range of which Pilot Mountain is part: Mount Brett and Massive Mountain.

The summit is also a classic place to rest and have lunch. An advantage of Silver being such a large dog is that he can carry supplies. I had made up a kind of cross between dog vest and saddlebags for him, so that he could carry his own water, food, and treats. As we sat enjoying the food, water, rest, and views – in that order – there was one thing that gave me pause.

"Don, have a look at those clouds," I said, pointing to one end of the Bow Valley, which was obscured by clouds.

"Mmm hmm. They look a bit threatening, don't they?"

"Yes. I could barely see them when we arrived, and already there are more of them and they're turning dark. It looks like it's raining or snowing over there too."

"The pressure's dropping fast too," I said, having consulted my altimeter[9]. "Storm's coming our way."

"Looks like it's still quite a way off. Can't tell whether it's rain or snow, but it's certainly dark," said Don, peering through his small binoculars.

"Mmm. When I took my mountaineering classes, our mountain guide always warned us about how deceptively fast storms can roll down the mountain valleys, and about how the worst places to get caught are on the summits and the rocky faces above the tree line."

"If you're suggesting this is a good time to start back, I agree," said Don, reaching for his daypack.

We made our descent mostly by retracing the path of our ascent, except for a few places where it had only been with hindsight that we discovered we'd climbed up slopes that were more difficult than they needed to be. As we approached the tree line, we had to back up and circle a bit before we found the brightly-coloured flags we'd left on the way up, but once we found them, we had no trouble finding the entrance to the path we'd ascended through the forest.

Just before entering the forest itself, we took a last look at the storm clouds while we could.

"They're coming our way," said Don. "I think we'll get back to the lodge well before the storm arrives, but it was a good call starting down when we did."

I agreed and, as it happened, we were unexpectedly delayed getting back.

A scream from behind us caused us to stop and turn.

"That didn't sound good," said Don.

"No," I agreed. "We'd better go have a look."

With us facing the mountain, we judged that the scream had come from ahead and to our left, whereas the route we'd taken earlier went off to our right. As we navigated our way up and left, it wasn't long before we could see the brightly-coloured jackets of several hikers. They seemed to be at the base of a steep rock face.

Our first impression was confirmed as we got closer, and the jackets resolved themselves into red, yellow, green, and red. It was, respectively, Gary, Pat, Gerry, and Kate.

By the time we reached them, we could see that the four of them were watching Barry and Dianne, who were kneeling beside Sandra, who was lying down and clearly had been hurt.

Dianne had clearly taken charge, and was instructing Barry to support Sandra in various ways while she examined her.

While the examination was underway, Pat explained that it had been her scream that we'd heard.

"We were taking turns climbing up the rock face here. For practice, you know?"

I looked at the rock face. There was a very broad chute, with pillars on each side, and the face was nearly vertical. It did however, have a wide array of projecting hand- and toe-holds and would be an easy climb for an experienced mountaineer or a good practice wall for someone learning to climb.

"Everyone else had already gone up, leaving just Sandra," Pat continued. "It's not hard to climb, but Sandra can be pretty timid sometimes, and she was nervous and wanted to give it a miss. Everyone else was excited, though, and shouting encouragement, so she gave it a try... She almost made it too. She was just a few feet below where someone could have given her a hand up when it happened.

"I could see her hands shaking," Pat continued, "like they

always do these days. Then she seemed to lose her nerve because her whole body began trembling. Then she missed a handhold, lost her balance, and fell... That's when I screamed. It was horrible! I could see the terror in her eyes when she lost her handhold and then her foothold."

The tears came then, and Gerry put his arms around her and led her off to one side.

By this time, Dianne had finished her examination and stood up to stretch her back.

"She's unconscious, she's broken a few bones, and I'm concerned there may be damage to her spinal cord. We're going to need a stretcher so we can immobilize her neck and carry her back."

"Will they have a stretcher way up here?" asked Barry.

"If they don't, they'll at least have the rescue sleds that the ski patrol uses in winter," I offered. "They're either fibreglass or aluminum, so there are enough of us to carry it without jostling her around."

"Good," said Dianne.

"I'll go," said Gary, who was easily the biggest and strongest.

"I'll come too," volunteered Don, who was the next strongest.

When they left, Dianne went back to sit with Barry, who hadn't left Sandra's side, while Silver and I went and sat with Pat, Gerry, and Kate to wait.

Waiting is hard, and with nothing else to do but think, it wasn't surprising that their thoughts would turn to guilt over having pushed Sandra to attempt a climb she hadn't wanted to make. Not wanting to make things worse, I kept my thoughts to myself, but as I gazed at the rock face, I couldn't help thinking that my old climbing instructor would not have let us free-climb such a face without precautions. It provided a good wall for practice climbing, but dangerous enough that you'd want to rig a top rope and have each climber in turn tied into the rope while one of their partners was on belay[10].

As we sat there, Gerry noticed that I was periodically looking at the clouds gathering above us. "What are you looking at?" he asked.

"The clouds. We noticed that the barometric pressure was dropping pretty quickly when we were up on the summit, and we could see the clouds gathering and darkening down at the end of the valley. That's why we were headed back when we were – to avoid the storm. Have you noticed that the wind has turned cold?" I looked at the small thermometer that was clipped to the zipper pull on my jacket. "It's down to zero now (0°C, 32°F), the clouds have caught up with us already, and now they seem to be getting darker the longer we're up here."

That peaked Gerry the physicist's interest. "May I see your altimeter?"

"Sure." I dug it out of my jacket pocket, along with my topo map. Handing him the altimeter, I showed him where we were on the map so he could reset the correct altitude, which allowed him to read off the pressure.

He whistled. "Very low, and this valley acts like a chute. There's nothing to stop that weather front from barreling right down the valley. Come to think of it, the wind has been feeling chillier too. Probably moisture." He thought about it a bit more, and then said, "I think we're in for a blast of snow."

I nodded. "As soon as the guys get back with the stretcher we'll want to clear out as soon as we can."

Time passes slowly when you're waiting, but it wasn't all that long before Gary and Don returned, bearing one of the ski patrol's aluminum rescue sleds. They'd had the presence of mind to also find some ropes and blankets, so that, under Dianne's direction they were able to pad the sled, load Sandra, cover her well, and tie her in. Dianne braced and secured Sandra's head and neck herself, not trusting anyone else to do that part properly because of the potential spinal injury.

By trial and error, we found that the makeshift stretcher was easiest to carry and keep stable with four bearers, rather than all eight of us, because of the rough terrain. So, that job fell to the four guys. Pat and I took the lead, having the jobs of finding the right trail back and watching out for places where the guys might lose their footing. Dianne and Kate brought up the rear.

Even though I'd been watching the storm clouds advance and settle over us, I was still surprised how dark it became, and how quickly.

The wind was picking up too, and it was definitely getting colder!

We were probably halfway to the lodge when it began to snow.

What began as a gentle, light snow with a bit of gentle, chill breeze soon became a full-blown snow-storm. By the time we reached the lodge, the combination of darkness, falling snow, and blowing wind had severely reduced visibility.

The storm had become a blizzard and temperature had continued to drop: it was already down to -5°C (+23°F).

As we passed through the lodge's big front doors, the bearers gently lowered the sled and we all brushed the snow off of our heads and jackets, I felt relieved that we had been able to get in when we had. Another half hour up above the tree-line and we'd have risked getting lost altogether in the forest – not a pleasant thought for any of us, let alone poor Sandra.

My relief was short lived, however. We were just beginning to explain to the resort manager what had happened, as a prelude to asking for help getting Sandra out and down to a hospital, when the power went out.

It wasn't yet late enough in the day for genuine darkness, but the sun was already blocked by the mountain and the increasing cloud cover made it darker than it otherwise would have been. The combination created a kind of grey atmosphere that was only slightly improved by the appearance of several battery-powered lanterns that were quickly set up in the lobby.

Marcel Gerrard, the young-looking manager of the resort was very embarrassed. He assured us that, although they only rarely experienced power outages, they had generator power to provide backup power for the most critical things, like food.

He explained that, "there's enough backup power to keep low-level emergency lights running throughout the resort, the heating system running at a low fan speed, and the kitchen refrigerators running, but not the big walk-in freezer. The heating system is powered by natural gas, as are the various fireplaces, and the ovens and ranges of the kitchen... and water is fed from a large water tank placed higher up on the mountain, So, we're OK for most things," he concluded

"Where does the power come from?" someone asked.

"It comes from two large diesel generators. They should have switched on automatically," he explained. "I've sent someone to go and have a look at them."

"What about the gondola?" asked Dianne.

"Its power is out too, and we don't have backup power for that. The size of generator required would have been cost prohibitive. The only other ways we can get people and supplies up and down the mountain is by a narrow road that runs all the way up."

Marcel offered Dianne the use of the Aid Station, that was used by the ski patrol during ski season, until the power was restored and the gondola was back in operation. So that's where Sandra was taken, accompanied by several of us carrying gas lanterns.

As we walked down a long, dark corridor more battery-powered lanterns created splashes of light and shadow on the walls and ceiling. It was both sombre and a bit spooky, and I think that it was the atmosphere that induced me to replay in my mind what Don and I had encountered.

Odd that a bunch of people that obviously care for her would encourage Sandra to climb a rock wall when she seemed to be so timid, shaky, and uncoordinated, I thought to myself. I decided that I was being overly suspicious, however, and put it out of my mind.

When we reached the Aid Station, Dianne examined Sandra again and pronounced her unchanged. "I'm still getting no eye-opening responses, no verbal responses, and no motor responses. I hope to be able to learn more when she starts showing some responsiveness or, better yet, when she regains consciousness."

"When will that be?" asked Barry.

"There's no way to tell," she answered. "Could be minutes or hours… if we're lucky."

"Lucky!" exclaimed Barry.

"This is serious, Barry. She's in a coma. Until something changes, all we can do is keep her comfortable and under observation."

Barry looked as if he was about to argue when, suddenly, the emergency lights came on. *They aren't bright, but they will at least keep people from running into the walls*, I thought.

"OK, at least now we can move around again," Marcel was saying, as he walked into the room.

He'd no sooner spoken these words, when the generators suddenly quit and the lights went out again.

"Damn," said Marcel, making an abrupt about-face and hastening back out of the room.

As the rest of us all just stood there for a moment, looking at each other, the only sounds to be heard were the hissing of the gas lanterns.

***

It was a sombre scene at supper that night. The blizzard had, if anything, become worse and the howling of the winds now dominated over the hushed conversations.

The emergency lighting just barely provided enough light for us to see what we were eating, and we'd just about finished our meals when Marcel came to inform us that a phone call to the power company had revealed that the storm had caused several sub-stations to fail, causing power blackouts all along the Bow Valley.

"The whole area has gotten up to 45 cm (18") of snow already, the highway has been closed to traffic and, it's still snowing out there. Given the amount of snow coming down," continued Marcel, "they're not optimistic about getting repair crews out to the sub-stations before tomorrow afternoon... If the snow lets up, that is."

Before anyone could ask, he quickly moved on to the next topic. "And, our big diesel generators have chosen this particular day to not cooperate. You'll have noticed that they cut out every once in a while."

"Murphy's Law[11]," said someone.

"What's happened?" asked Gary.

"We're not sure. One of the lift attendants is pretty handy with mechanical things, so we made him responsible for the generators. But he's not exactly an expert on the things. One of the problems is that the generators are in a shed with open windows all around, and the blizzard is making it hard for him to actually do anything."

"Sounds like we're going to be depending on those generators for a while, and you have two engineers here," said Don, nodding towards Gary, who immediately nodded back. "Would it be OK if we offered to help?"

"It sure would! If you would like to finish eating and then grab some warm clothes and meet me at the main reception desk, I'll take you there and introduce you to Kevin, the lift attendant. He's a good fellow and will appreciate the help."

Marcel left us then, looking somewhat relieved, and after a few more minutes Don and Gary excused themselves to go and get their coats and boots. As they were taking their first few steps, Gary was just passing an unoccupied table when he suddenly swore and bent over to rub his ankle.

"Did you run into a table leg?" asked Pat.

"Damn it all! No, I think I was attacked by that monster cat. Look here."

Pulling out a chair, Gary lifted one trouser leg to show everyone a couple of parallel, bleeding scratches.

It must have been Merlin, of course, hiding underneath the table and concealed by the white linen tablecloths that the staff had placed on the tables to dress them up for dinner. I say 'must have been' because whomever the perpetrator was had quickly and silently vanished from the scene.

As Don and Gary left the room, with Gary still muttering curses about cats in general, the server told us that Merlin liked to hide anywhere he could conceal himself and then reach out and swipe at the ankles of any human foolish enough to come within reach.

Everyone one immediately took sides, with Dianne and Kate expressing irritation that the management would allow a savage cat to roam freely about the place. This was surprising given that Kate had two cats of her own at home.

On the other side, Pat and I were unsuccessful at suppressing our urges to laugh, as we both thought it was funny that Merlin would take on the largest man on the hill and get away with it. Gary, after all, was too tough a man to be genuinely hurt by the scratches, and my impression was that he was too good a person to hold a grudge after his initial irritation had subsided.

Pat and I also apparently shared the same taste in literature, as we both appreciated the similarity of the event to things attributed to a fictional cat named Macavity, the principal character in the T. S. Eliot poem *Macavity: The Mystery Cat*[12].

No one remained for much longer in the dining room. Barry was looking quite pale and continued to worry and ask Dianne questions about Sandra. Pat made numerous attempts to distract the others from their worries with new, lighter topics of conversation but only Gerry, her boyfriend, seemed to appreciate her efforts. Dianne, for her part, maintained a determined stoicism as if she was determined not to let her sister's crisis break down her physician's cool and detached professional manner.

It was an act though. Although she displayed perfect control of her outward manner, particularly body and voice, I could see the turmoil in her eyes. If any further evidence of this was needed, it came when she finally lost her temper with Barry's incessant questions and said, rather sharply, "I keep telling you. There's nothing more anyone can do right now besides wait until something changes with Sandra or someone fixes that damn gondola so we can get her to a hospital." With that, she rose from the table and stalked off in the direction of the Aid Station where one of the resort staff had been pressed into service keeping an eye on the patient.

"Don't let her get to you Barry," offered Pat. "It's only natural that you're so concerned."

"I'd like to see her show some concern," muttered Barry.

"She's just playing the detached, analytical physician," said Kate. "I'm sure that deep down, she's just as worried about Sandra as you are."

"If she can be this cold to her own sister," growled Barry, unconvinced, "then I'd hate to see how she treats her other patients." With that he too rose from the table and stalked off.

"Why don't we go sit somewhere more comfortable?" suggested Pat. "You're welcome to join us Alex, if you'd like."

"Thanks, but I think I'd better go check on Silver," I replied. As the others rose and headed towards the resort's TV lounge, I went the other way, to our rooms.

After lounging for about an hour, and with no sign of Don, I decided to take Silver for a walk. I didn't want to risk getting lost in the blizzard, however, so we stayed close to the walls of the lodge and circled its perimeter. When we'd made our way along the entire front of the lodge, we came to the gondola station, which we circled. This brought us around to the rear of the lodge, where there were some storage sheds and the generator shack.

The generator shack was hard to miss, as it was the source of a lot of hammering sounds. When we reached the shack, we found Don and Gary busily building the last of a series of makeshift windows. They had nailed a number of wood slats across the last open window and were in the process of doubling up a white bed sheet, which they used to cover the slats. Then they nailed the sheet into place, and began to cover it with another layer of wooden slats, which were placed perpendicular to inside ones.

"What do you think?" asked Don, as he stepped back with Gary to admire their handiwork. "We couldn't do anything in there between the wind and the snow beginning to pile up, so we took apart some old pallets to get the wood slats, and raided the laundry for the sheets."

"Very resourceful. Reminds me a bit of a prospector's shelter," I said.

"It'll do," said Gary. "The generators weren't vented, so we rigged up vents using aluminum tape and spare ventilation tubing from the lodge's clothes dryers." He showed me where two sets of dryer tubing snaked across the room, supported by wires from the ceiling, and exiting through holes cut into large pieces of cardboard. "The tubing just barely made it to the wall, but it's enough to get the exhaust gases out so we don't get a buildup of carbon monoxide."

"Doesn't the open doorway provide enough ventilation?" I asked.

"Not for long it won't," said Gary. "There's a mechanical shop of sorts in the gondola station. Kevin's in there right now making us a door. Let's go see how he's doing."

Walking back to the gondola station, we entered a back door that I hadn't previously noticed, which opened onto the mechanical shop. Although this was a fairly large room, about a third of it was taken up by a curving track attached to the ceiling, from which was suspended a gondola car that had obviously been brought in for some kind of maintenance or repair. The rest of the room was filled with tool chests, workbenches, power tools, and welding equipment. Leading us over to one of the workbenches, Gary introduced me to Kevin Beach, the lift attendant and generator steward.

"Hi!" said Kevin, straightening up from his work. He looked to be about eighteen years old, sported a shock of blond hair and a brilliant smile, and seemed to have the outgoing personality to match. "I've gone from lift attendant, to generator operator, to carpenter, all in one day," he said, pointing to the workbench. On the bench were two wooden doors, lying flat and placed edge to edge. He had attached a pivoting metal plate to one and a U-shaped receiver for it to the other door.

"We found two spare bedroom doors in one of the storage sheds. The two of them will easily cover the doorway in the generator shack. I've reversed the hinges on one, and rigged up this metal plate so it can be swung up to open the doors, and swung down into this receiver to close them."

"Good work," congratulated Don. "Let's go try them out."

With two people to carry each door, it was easy to take them over to the generator shack and install one on each side of the broad doorway, using the screws that Kevin had brought with him.

I had to stifle a smile as we all stepped back to look at the installed doors, the guys with pride and me with amusement. What they saw, was a makeshift, but serviceable double door. What I saw was a pair of mismatched doors, in rather garish and clashing colours, sporting in the middle a roughly rectangular slab of rusty metal.

"Did you find out why the generators kept quitting?" I asked.

"Oh yes," said Gary. "The driving snow was coming in, melting, and seeping into the boxes for the power transfer switch and the circuits leading to the lodge. The seeping water was causing electrical shorts that caused the circuit breakers to trip."

"So that's why you've added the makeshift windows and doors."

"Right," said Kevin. "We shouldn't have any more troubles after this."

He was so wrong.

Laurie Schramm

5 CUT OFF

Day 4: Monday, October 22, 1979

Other than a natural concern for Sandra's condition, Don and I were still having a good time. Despite the storm, we still had the fresh mountain air, it was quite peaceful, the food was good, and we were away from work.

Before breakfast, Pat suggested that we go check on Sandra, so I left Silver with Don and accompanied her and Kate. Sandra had been moved back to her room, into which Barry had dragged the mattress from his room so that he could be nearby without disturbing her. Both Barry and Dianne were there with her when we arrived.

"Any change?" asked Pat.

"No, but things are no worse, and it's early yet. Time will tell us more," replied Dianne.

Breakfast, of course, was another sombre affair for the group of friends, but this time because of concern for Sandra. When they were seated at their usual tables, we overheard Dianne reporting that there had been no change in Sandra's condition overnight.

Their mood wasn't helped when Marcel, the resort manager, stopped by to announce to us all that the blizzard had continued through the night. This didn't come as a surprise to any of us that had arisen and looked out our bedroom windows. Silver and I, in fact, had already been out for a walk and he had a great time leaping and playing in the fresh snow banks.

What was news was the weather forecast, which called for continued blizzard conditions that were not forecast to ease until the end of the day at the earliest, and more likely not for the whole next day after that.

Don looked at me and smiled. I knew what he was thinking: a couple of days of being snow-bound weren't really going to affect our plans all that much.

"What about the power?" asked Barry.

"The backup generator ran perfectly all night long, and is still running right now, thanks to your and Kevin's work on the generator shed last night. The main power is going to remain off until the power company's crews can get to the damaged substations, but no one seems to know when the roads will be opened again. Fortunately, we have a good supply of food and diesel fuel."

"And the gondola?" asked Dianne.

"We don't have enough power to run the gondola and, in any case, there's no point. The lower-station crew went home to Banff last night, when the police warned that they were about to close the highway which, of course, is still closed."

"Is there no other way we can get Sandra to a hospital?" asked Barry.

"I'm afraid not," apologized Marcel. "I thought of calling the hospital or the park wardens to see if we could get a helicopter, or a snow-cat, or even snowmobiles and toboggans in as far as the lower gondola station…" he sighed. "But I'm afraid that the phone line went dead overnight too. The storm must have taken down some telephone poles, somewhere. The only news we're getting is what we can hear from the radio. Other than that, I'm afraid we're completely cut off for the time being."

But Barry didn't give up that easily. "How about going out by snowmobile?"

"Yes, we could do that," said Marcel. Seeing Kevin, the lift attendant, walking by he waved him over and introduced him to those that had not met him the night before.

"Kevin, what would you think about someone taking one of our snowmobiles and running into town to see if we can get help for the young woman that was injured yesterday."

Kevin thought for a moment. "We could pull one of the rescue sleds and take her right to the hospital, but with all this powder snow you'd have to keep some speed up to prevent the snowmobile from sinking into the snow. That would make it a bumpy ride for anyone with a suspected spinal injury."

All heads turned to look at Dianne, who shook her head, saying, "Out of the question."

"Right then. We can still send someone – two people, for safety – down to Banff to let the park wardens know what's going on up here, and so they can get us some kind of help as soon as possible... After the blizzard lets up of course," continued Kevin. "Do you want me to go? George the handyman knows how to run the generators."

"No, I think we should keep you here so we have more than one person to look after them."

"Are you sure? I have the most experience touring around on the machines anyway, and I know the route well enough to find my way even with everything covered in snow."

Before Marcel could reply, Gary piped up, saying, "I think I can handle the generator now. Kevin's shown me how it works and I've already helped him refuel the tank from the diesel drums."

"Thank you, Gary, that's very good of you," said Marcel. "OK then, Kevin, you're elected to go, but we'll need a second person to go with you on a second snow mobile, for safety. Do any of you have snowmobiling experience?" Marcel asked, looking around the room.

Don and I were considering whether to volunteer when Gerry beat us to it.

"I'll go," he said. "I've done a lot of snowmobiling in Ontario and Quebec. What kind of machines do you have?"

"1979 Ski-Doo Everest 444s with extra-wide skis. They're very solid, with 50 hp engines," said Kevin.

"Sounds fine. How long a ride will it be?"

"Well, it's 5 km down the mountain, then 8 km from the lower gondola station to the highway, and then 21 km along the highway to Banff. That makes it about 34 km. We'll be able to ride on the roads all the way, so poor visibility shouldn't be too much of a problem for us. It'll be slow riding in fresh powder, but fun... and tiring! If we leave this morning, we'll have lots of time, even allowing for breaks."

"OK, but take the survival packs in case you hit white-out conditions and have to stop," said Marcel.

"Right," agreed Kevin. "Come on Gerry, I'll find you a snow-suit and helmet and show you the machines."

"Is there anything you need brought back up here, Doctor?" Marcel asked Dianne.

"No, not really. The intravenous supplies you have in stock for the paramedics provide enough to keep her glucose and hydration up. Beyond that, all I can do for now is monitor Sandra's respiration and circulation, until something changes."

After breakfast, most of us went out to see the snowmobilers off. It was somewhat reassuring to see that most of the blizzard had blown itself out, at least where we were. There was still a light snow coming down, but the wind was much reduced and visibility was more than sufficient for Gerry and Kevin who headed off with a wave and the roar of engines.

It had been agreed that we weren't to worry if they were not back by dark. If roads turned out to be slow-going, then the plan was for them to stay in Banff overnight and come back next day.

While we were outside, this was the first time that Silver was introduced to Dianne. Not that Dianne was at all interested, but Gary insisted on introducing them. Perhaps it was because Dianne was so uninterested, but Silver didn't take a liking to her either. Not that he barked or growled at her, he didn't, but his body stiffened a bit and the hair on the back of his neck bristled. I found it interesting that he reacted so differently to the various friends in this group but didn't think more about it until much later.

The rest of the day was spent lounging about the lodge, with most people choosing to read or watch TV. It seemed somewhat bizarre to be cut off from the rest of the world, with not even a working phone line, and yet be able to watch TV. This was made possible by the fact that the resort had purchased one of the new – and very expensive – satellite TV systems, with its huge, 4.9 m (16 ft.) diameter dish mounted prominently-high-up, behind the lodge. With this dish, it was possible to receive signals from some of the eighteen communications satellites in geostationary orbit high up above the Earth.

Don and I spent the rest of the morning in the main lounge, where we had a nice chat with Pat and Gary. They both had such lively, outgoing personalities that the time passed quickly. After that, we had lunch in our suite and spent the afternoon with Silver in the suite, reading.

***

Meanwhile, Kevin and Gerry were working their way towards Banff. They had a little trouble navigating the winding road down Pilot Mountain because of poor visibility caused by the driving snow. It wasn't a total whiteout but they had to be careful, even with Kevin, who knew the road well, in the lead. Complicating matters was the fact that in several places banks of fresh powder adjoined banks of hard, wind-blown snow. It was not always obvious where such intersections occurred, and crossing from hard to soft snow, or the reverse, often caused the snowmobiles to jerk and twist. As a result, there were several occasions in which Gerry lost control of his machine and tipped over into the softer snow. Gerry knew enough to throw him self off of the machine when he'd lost control of it, so that the heavy machine couldn't land on top of him. As a result, the only injuries were to his pride. Each time Kevin noticed that Gerry had tipped over he would stop his machine and walk back along the newly packed track made by his own machine. Typically, by the time he had walked back to check on Gerry, the latter was still working to extricate himself from a bank of waist-deep power.

Although the soft landings didn't cause Gerry any injury, each time it happened it took both Gerry and Kevin to right the heavy machine and get it back onto the track created by Kevin's machine, so they could continue. This was both time-consuming and exhausting for both of them.

When they reached the lower gondola station, they took advantage of the station to make a rest stop where it was warm and dry, before continuing down the road that led to the highway. Once on the main highway, the winds were less gusty and less forceful, and the visibility improved slightly. It was also a much simpler matter to ride down the centre of the highway where the snow was uniform and there were no hidden obstacles in their way. As a result, or perhaps due to his increasing confidence riding the machine, Gerry had no further incidents of tipping over.

There was one other incident, however. Following one of their rest stops, the drive belt on Gerry's snowmobile broke when he was attempting to restart it. There was a spare in each machine, and Kevin demonstrated how to replace it. Despite this, they were unable to restore the proper tension to the belt, with the result that the machine remained inoperable.

"I think it's time to throw in the towel on this field repair," said Keven, eventually. "There's a tow cable in my machine, but we'll never be able to have you double-up with me on my machine plus tow yours in all this powder. Let's just tow yours over to the side of the highway, and then we can ride into town on my machine, together."

The single machine was able to carry both men over the powder snow, but between the reduced speed and all of the days stops and delays, it was the end of the afternoon before they reached Banff.

Day 5: Tuesday, October 23, 1979

Before breakfast the next morning, Don and I went to check on Sandra's condition. When we reached her room, Pat and Kate were already there on the same mission.

"Things are improving," Dianne was saying, as we walked in. "During the night, she finally started responding to external stimuli: opening her eyes, and making some sounds and movements. Barry says that she's started moaning or murmuring once in a while on her own, and that her eyes seemed to be moving a bit underneath her lids."

"Are you still worried about a possible spinal injury?" I asked.

"Not so much. She seems to be able to move her head a little on her own. We'll know more if she continues to come out of the coma."

It was very sobering, standing there watching Sandra just lying there in bed, attached to an intravenous tube, knowing that she might never regain consciousness. But then we all got a surprise when Kate went over, kissed her on the forehead, and said, "Come on Sandra, you can beat this thing!"

Sandra's eyes immediately popped open, and she moved one arm as if to raise her hand towards Kate before it suddenly fell back beside her on the bed.

"She's awake!" gasped Barry.

"Not yet!" said Dianne, rather sharply, watching Sandra closely. "She can't focus her eyes yet. See how they seem to be staring into space. And her arm movement may have been random, despite how it appeared."

"But this is a good sign, right...? Progress?"

"Yes, it's a good sign." Dianne finally gave a tight smile. "It's a very good sign, but we're not out of the woods yet."

Pat went over and gave Barry a reassuring touch on his shoulder as we took our leave.

As we walked down the hallway together, I noticed that Kate was shaking her hand up and down, as if to dislodge something.

"What's that?" I asked.

"Something stuck to my fingers... It's hair. There were some hairs lying loose on Sandra's pillow, a few of them must have become stuck to my fingers."

"Were there many of them?"

"Many of what...? Oh, hairs? Yes, there were some on each side of her head. Maybe underneath too. I couldn't tell. Some of them must have been pulled out when she fell and hit her head."

"Yes, that must be it," I said, in a neutral voice. At least I hoped it was a neutral voice, because a little tiny alarm bell had just gone off in the back of my own head. Something about hair falling out seemed familiar somehow, but I couldn't place it at the time. I did, however, make a mental note to give it more thought.

After breakfast there still wasn't much that we could do outside, so Don and Silver and I spent the morning in our suite resting and reading in front of our fireplace.

When I went to visit Sandra in the early afternoon, there were further signs that she was slowly getting better. Barry, who had rarely left her side since the accident, was showing some signs of life, which was explained by his first words: "She's getting better!"

"That's great," I said, as I walked over to her bed for a look.

As I chatted with Barry and Diane, I could see that Sandra's eyes were opening more often, and I noticed that her head would sometimes turn in response to sights and sounds.

"Yes, she's starting to be able to track sights and sounds," said Dianne in confirmation. "She doesn't seem to recognize what she's seeing or hearing yet, but it's a good sign."

"Can you tell anything about brain damage yet?" I asked.

"No. If she continues to improve, then the next stage will be an ability to recognize things that are happening to her, and to follow commands more or less consistently. After that, there will be a period in which she takes in what's going on around her but will seem confused, have trouble with her memory, and trouble controlling her body, arms, and legs. That will be scary for the others, especially for Barry here, but it'll be a good sign anyway because it's part of the process."

"Any idea how long that will take?" I asked.

"No. There's no way to predict how long it will take, or how much she'll actually recover. We just have to take it one step at a time."

Dianne seemed to be spending as much time consoling Barry as she did in watching over Sandra, so I decided she had enough on her hands and took my leave.

***

Some time later, Barry left his vigil and walked down the long hallway towards the main lodge building.

Not long after this, a shadowy figure entered Sandra's room. Although the curtains were drawn and it was quite dark, the figure knew the layout well and had no trouble silently crossing to her bed.

As they approach, Sandra's eyes open wide as she recognizes the figure, and for the first time since the accident she speaks coherently.

"What happened?"

"You were climbing the rock face on the mountain. You fell and hit your head. Do you remember?"

Sandra's eyes take on a vacant look for a moment, then suddenly go back into focus. "I knew I couldn't do it. You pushed me into that!"

"Yes, but everything's going to be OK now," said the figure as their hands reached out toward Sandra's face, caressing it once from each side. Then, one hand moved up and pinched her nose closed while the other clamped down hard on Sandra's mouth, holding it shut as well.

Sandra instinctively tried to twist her body and raise her hands to ward off the unexpected attack, but with her motor control still unrecovered her body only twitches, while her arms were only able to shake and flail about in random directions. As she began to suffocate, her arm movements became stronger, but still ineffective.

Her body held out for almost a minute before lack of oxygen caused it to begin shutting down and she lost consciousness. In another six minutes she was beyond any possibility of resuscitation.

Releasing their grip, the figure's hands caressed Sandra's face once more before the figure stood up, turned and, with an air of casual assurance, slipped out of the room the way they had come.

The figure had been in the room for less than nine minutes.

About twenty minutes later, Barry returned to the suite and went to check on Sandra.

***

Don, Silver and I were lounging in our suite, and I was just about to suggest we go outside for a walk when we heard a male voice yell for help.

"Sounds close," said Don. "Barry, next door maybe?"

"Let's go see," I said, and we all rushed out into the hall and tried knocking on Barry and Sandra's suite, which was next to ours.

"Barry, is that you?" Don called.

"Yes, in here. Quick!" came the reply.

The door wasn't locked, so we went in and found Barry in Sandra's room. He was stretched over top of Sandra's chest, giving her CPR[13], with his hands stacked, fingers interlocked, the heel of one hand placed on her chest, and his arms locked straight.

"I came in – twenty - and found her breathing - twenty-one - had stopped - - twenty-two - and no pulse," said Barry, speaking in short bursts as he continued to give chest compressions and maintain his count. When he reached thirty, he switched over to Sandra's head, adjusted its tilt with one hand and her chin with the other, leaned in and gave her two rescue breaths. We could see Sandra's chest rise and fall with each breath.

"Her airway's clear," said Barry, as he moved back to resume chest compressions, restarting his count. "One... two... three..."

As he did, Don moved over to position himself on the other side of Sandra's body, saying, "I'll do the next breaths when the count's up."

"What's going on?" asked Dianne, as she and Pat entered the room.

"Barry says he came in and found her not breathing and with no pulse," I explained. "He yelled for help, and we just got here a couple of minutes ago."

"OK. Everyone move back so I can take a look," she ordered, "and get that damn dog out of here!"

At this, the hair on Silver's neck bristled and he gave a menacing growl, but I grabbed his collar and hustled him out of the room.

The rest I learned from Don when he came back into our rooms about half an hour later.

"It's no good," he reported. "After checking Sandra over, Dianne had Barry continue the CPR while she ran down to the Aid Station for some adrenaline and a syringe. When she got back, she injected shots of adrenaline into a vein every few minutes or so, while Barry continued the compressions and I did the rescue breaths. Eventually, Dianne told us to stop, that there was nothing more we could do for her."

"How are the others?"

"Barry's exhausted and pretty broken-up. Dianne is her usual stoic self. She thanked Pat and I, and Kate – who'd also come in to see if she could help. Then she asked us to give the two of them some time alone. When we left, Dianne had sat Barry down on the couch and had her arms around him. I think they're going to need some time."

"Such a horrible thing. I think everyone will need some time to deal with this."

"Including us. How about that walk?" asked Don.

"I can't believe it's still snowing!" I exclaimed as we went outside. "It feels like it will never end."

The wind had almost completely abated, however, which made it seem like progress of a sort.

"They won't be able to clear the roads very quickly, much less fix the power for a while yet," said Don. "Maybe by tomorrow we'll hear about some progress."

As we walked, we once again kept the lodge and its outbuildings in sight which meant we could only walk the perimeter. As we walked around the rear of the lodge, we were greeted by the reassuring sound of the generator working away in its enclosed shed.

"Do you know how much diesel fuel is stored up here?" I asked.

"According to Kevin, they had enough for a week when the power went out. So, we should be good for three more days, but I'm sure things will be up and running again before that."

"Could have been worse," I mused, thoughtfully. "I wouldn't want to be caught up here with no heat and power."

"Me neither but even then, this place would be pretty luxurious compared to the time we spent in tents out in The Barrens when it was fifty degrees colder[14]."

That made me shiver. "Don't remind me! Even Silver minded that cold."

On that note, we went back inside for supper.

It was a sombre affair in the dining room that evening. The only diners were Don and I at one table and Gary, Pat, and Kate at another. When we went in, Pat told us that Barry hadn't felt like eating, and that Dianne had stayed back to try to console him.

The one thing that amused me, at least, was after supper when we made to leave the dining room. As we were walking by one of the tables, a paw snuck out from under the long-hanging tablecloth and took a swipe at Don's ankle. It only grazed his angle enough for him to notice it, however, but Don immediately reached down and lifted the tablecloth. Merlin, for it could only have been him, was – like the fictional Macavity – nowhere to be seen. He had made his mark, however. When the others rose to leave the dining room, I noticed that everyone took care not to walk close to any of the covered tables.

Chuckling, Don and I returned to our rooms and settled in with Silver, in front of the fireplace in our suite.

***

Later that night, Gary went out to refill the diesel tanks on the generators. This took a while because he had to use a hand truck to manoeuvre a fresh barrel of diesel fuel over to the first generator, unscrew the bung cap with a specially made wrench, then replace the cap with a bung adapter, which was needed for attaching the pump. The hand-crack-style pump was mounted on top of a steel pipe that was slightly less long than the height of the drum. Gary inserted the long pipe into the barrel then screwed the base of the pump into the bung adapter. The pump had a flexible hose connected to its outlet, which Gary led to the opening of the generator's fuel tank. After inserting the hose into the tank, he then had to stand beside the diesel drum and turn the hand crank. At the rate he was cranking the pump it would take about eight minutes, then he would have to switch in a second barrel and begin the whole procedure again, in order to fill the 95 U.S. gallon tank. After that, he would use two more barrels of fuel to fill the tank of the second generator.

It was hot in the generator shed. In order to keep the power on in the resort, Gary and Kevin had been taking the risk of hot-fueling the generators, meaning that they kept the generators running while simultaneously refilling their diesel tanks. As a result, Gary wasn't able to hear anything while the generators kept up their deafening roar. To make matters worse, with both fuel barrels and fuel tanks open while he was doing the filling, the air was full of the smell of diesel fuel.

Because of the intense fuel smell, Gray didn't smell any change when a shadowy figure approached the makeshift vent openings at the back of the generator shack, used a knife to slit the aluminum tape which was all that was holding them in place through the holes in the walls, and pushed them back inside, after which they promptly fell to the floor. Then, withdrawing a roll of the same kind of aluminum tape, the figure simply taped over the holes in the wall. This was quickly accomplished, as each hole only required three to four pieces of tape to span the opening.

The figure next walked around to the front of the shack and opened the door just a crack, but enough to be able to watch as Gary finished the first drum, then the second, then moved over to transfer fuel from a third drum to the second generator, and then began with the fourth. It was heavy work moving the drums around and constantly operating the hand pump so that, despite his size, strength, and fitness, the work, heat, and noise were considerably slowing him down.

As the figure continued to watch, Gary settled into the business of transferring fuel from the fourth barrel. In the middle of doing this, he began to shake his head from side to side as dizziness set in, but he put this down to a combination of heat and fatigue. Just a few more minutes and I'll be done, *he thought to himself. As he pumped the last of the fuel into the second generator, he thought - Finally! - because he was beginning to feel nauseous as well. He was noticeably unsteady on his feet as he attempted to unscrew and remove the hand-pump from the fourth barrel. This took several attempts before he got it right, but he finally managed it. He was in the process of using the hand-truck to move the empty barrel over beside its companions when he lost motor control completely and dropped to the floor.*

He could still have been saved, at that point, had someone found him and dragged him outside into the fresh air, but there was no one around but the shadowy figure that had caused the incident in the first place. For its part, the figure simply nodded its head once, opened the door and darted inside. Within two minutes the figure emerged carrying something in its arms, then went back around to the back of the shack to remove the tape from the two vent holes.

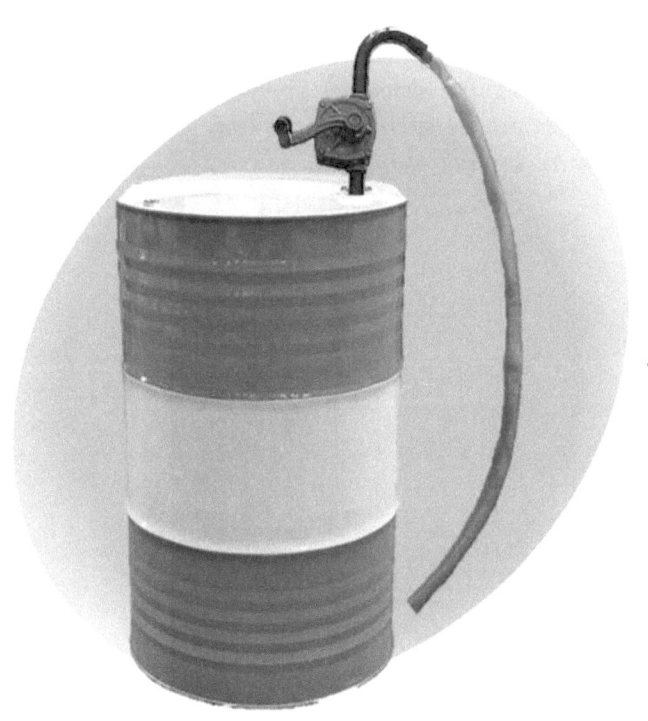

6 DUTY CALLS

Day 6: Wednesday, October 24, 1979

The next morning, we woke up to the sound of someone loudly knocking on the door to our suite. It was Marcel, the resort manager.

"Can you come with me please? There's been another death."

Many questions popped into my mind all at once but, with an effort, I held them back and simply said, "Sure."

Don wanted to come with me, and I decided to bring Silver as well. As the three of us followed Marcel, I was surprised that he led us outside to the generator shed. Leaving Don and Silver outside for the moment, Marcel and I went in.

There, lying between a barrel and one of the generators was Gary, wearing that paper-like look of death that always reminded me of the faces of unwrapped mummies.

I first went over to Dianne, who was sitting, hunched-over on an overturned bucket, with her head in her hands.

"Are you OK Dianne?"

"Yes, I'm fine. It's Gary. It's all my fault. When I went to bed last night, he said that he was going to come here and refuel the generators before turning-in himself. I should have come with him."

"How late was that?"

"Ten o'clock. I remember because I looked at the clock when he went out."

"Did you see or hear from him again after that?"

"No. Nothing. But when I got up this morning, I cleaned up a bit and then went over to his and Gerry's suite to see if he was ready for breakfast. When I got there, Gerry wasn't there, of course, and neither was Gary – and his bed hadn't been slept in either. That made me afraid, so I went to search for him, planning to begin with the generator shed. When I got here, the generators were running, the lights were still on, and I found him lying there like that." She pointed towards Gary's slumped figure. "He was already dead. No pulse, no respiration, a red, flushed skin colour, his body was cold, and rigor mortis was pretty well advanced."

"Red skin colour?"

"Yes, reddish skin colouring is an indicator of carbon monoxide poisoning. The red colour comes with elevated, usually fatal, levels of carboxyhemoglobin in the blood. It's because of that that I pushed out one of the window coverings and propped the door open. That was before I called Marcel."

"So, you checked on Gary, then pushed out the window covering and opened the door. Have you touched anything else?"

She looked around the shed. "I don't think so, no, other than grabbing this bucket to sit on after I brought Marcel in."

"And when did you say you last saw Gary?"

"Just before I went to bed at about ten o'clock."

"And… I'm sorry, but I have to ask. How long would you estimate that he has been dead?"

"Well, the air in the shed is hot but the floor is cold. Based on the degree of rigor mortis, I'd say at least eight hours ago – maybe. Six or more hours for sure."

"And after you got up, you went searching and found him like this at…?"

"About 20 minutes ago, so just after 9:30."

So, between 10 pm the night before and 3:30 am this morning, I thought to myself.

"Is it OK if I look around?" I asked Marcel.

"Whatever you need to do," he said, "and anything you need, just ask."

I was just about to begin looking around the shed when Barry stuck his head in the doorway and stopped short in shock, when he saw Gary. Then, collecting himself, he rushed over to Dianne and asked a rush of questions that included what had happened and whether she was OK.

"I'm OK," she said, "come back to the lodge, and I'll tell you." With a look towards me to confirm that that was OK, which I acknowledged, she led Barry out of the shed and, I assume, back to the lodge.

"Has anything else been touched?" I asked Marcel.

"Not as far as I know," he replied.

"Fine. Give me a few minutes to look around, then I'll come and find you."

"I'll be in my office," he replied then promptly left, presumably relieved to be able to get away from the sight of the body.

I asked Don if he would make a quick dash back to my room for my camera then I took a quick look around the inside of the generator shed, then went around and looked around the outside of the shed. While I did that Silver nosed around outside on his own.

The snow had finally stopped coming down at some time during the night, so it was easy to spot the tracks. There was a set of tracks coming from the lodge to the shed, but so many people had tramped back and forth that way that I didn't find any clues there. When Don returned with my camera, he found me examining two different sets of tracks in the snow, one that led from the door of the shed around the back to where the exhaust holes had been improvised, and the other leading from there right back to the shed's door.

"Whose tracks are those?" he asked.

"Good question. These tracks are pretty fresh. I think someone came back here last night, for some reason."

Don looked around. "I don't see anything interesting except those two vent holes that Kevin, Gary, and I made."

"I agree. Do you see anything different about those vent holes?"

"No, I don't..." began Don, as he walked over for a closer look. "Wait a minute, the vent hoses aren't attached any more!"

"Exactly. The hoses are lying on the floor inside, near the back wall."

"You mean the shed filled with exhaust fumes last night."

"Yes. But if someone walked back here last night, they must have either seen or known about the hoses coming free. And look at the prints in the snow. They were made by large boots."

"Yes," said Don. "I have pretty large feet, but those came from bigger feet than mine."

"Hmm. Hang on a moment, would you? And make sure that a few of these prints don't get trampled." Taking my camera, I went back into the generator shed and photographed Gary's body from different angles, including close-up and perspective shots. I am no forensic photographer, but I did the best I could. After that, I knelt down and took off one of Gary's boots. They were of the large, felt-pack type, comprising a large, waterproof outer boot with an all-terrain sole, plus an inner felt boot to provide the insulation. *Gary must have been the type to prepare for any contingency*, I thought to myself as I struggled to get a boot off, as such boots were designed to protect against the worst that a deep winter could provide, yet we were only into late fall.

It was as I was thinking about Gary's boot choice, that it occurred to me to wonder why such large boots were so difficult to get off. Then I took a closer look, and realized that the boots were on the wrong feet!

At the same moment, the boot came free and I took it back out and around to the back of the shed.

"Any trouble?" asked Don, having noticed that it had taken me longer than it should have.

"You could say that," I replied. "His boots were hard to get off. They were on the wrong feet."

Don just whistled, having immediately come to the same conclusion I had.

Crouching down beside a clear-looking boot-print, I compared it with the one in my hand. One looked like the mirror-image of the other. Then I tried placing the boot in one of the prints.

"Seems to fit perfectly," I remarked.

"You don't sound surprised," said Don. "You don't think Gary pushed the vent hoses back inside the shed by himself, to commit suicide, do you?"

"Anything's possible, I guess, but no. Do you?"

"Not at all. In fact, I'd have ranked him as the least likely suicide of the whole bunch, but that's just based on his outgoing, 'friendly bear' personality. Who knows what may have been going on in the depths of his mind?"

"I don't know what's going on here at all," I said, exasperated, "but two sudden deaths in two days, involving the same group of friends, seems like an unlikely coincidence."

Selecting an untouched boot-print in the snow, I placed the boot beside it, but lying on its side, then took pictures of the two together, and of each individually.

When I arose, I glanced around. That was when I noticed that Silver was over at the edge of the nearby forest, and had been digging at something.

"Silver?" I called, questioningly.

At that, Silver looked up at me, gave out a sharp "Bark," and sat on his haunches.

"Found something," I commented, as I rose. When Don and I had tramped through the snow to get to him I could see that, just inside the forest, he'd been digging a bit of a hole in the snow with his front paws.

"What have you found Silver?" I asked, rhetorically, as I bent down for a look.

Something crumpled and silvery. I grabbed my camera, took a few pictures, and then reached in for whatever it was.

"Two mushed up balls of aluminum tape stuck together," I said, standing up to show Don.

"Looks like the same kind of tape we used to attach the dryer vent hoses to the generator exhaust pipes and then to the hole we cut in the window coverings."

"Yes, and each ball of tape seems to be made up of a bunch of strips."

"Uh, oh," said Don, as the implications of this find sunk in.

"Uh, oh, is right. Let's keep this discovery to ourselves for now, OK? Same with the boot tracks... It doesn't look like anything else out here has attracted Silver's attention. Why don't we go back inside? I think we've learned as much as we can out here."

Then I went through the shed as carefully as I could and photographed everything I could think of, beginning with Gary's body. When viewed up close, I could see the red flush of his skin that Dianne mentioned. There were no signs of bruising or a struggle.

I did make one more discovery in the shed. The tape at the ends of the two hoses hadn't fallen inside on their own, nor had the tape used to hold them in place failed: the tape securing the hoses had clearly been cut with something sharp, like scissors or a knife.

"So, it wasn't an accident, and it wasn't suicide. It was murder," said Don when I was photographing the hose ends.

"Yes, these hoses didn't pull away by themselves. But, if people want to think that it was an accident, then we'll let them. For a little while at least."

On our way back to speak to Marcel, we stopped to check the boot racks at the lodge's entrance. Not surprisingly, all of the boots and shoes were of smaller sizes than Gary's.

"I didn't think we were likely to find any others of Gary's size," I commented to Don.

"Yes, I haven't yet seen anyone up here that's as large as Gary is… I mean, was," said Don. "That means that anyone here could have taken his boots off and used them to get to the back of the shed to sabotage the venting system – any of the guests, or any of the staff for that matter."

"I'm afraid so."

Don took Silver off with him to see about helping to reconnect the exhaust pipes in the generator shed. That left me free to find Marcel and ask him for the use of a room in which we could interview the staff.

For the rest of the morning, Marcel and I sat in a conference room near his office, the two of us sitting on one side of the conference table and a procession of staff members that were summoned one at a time. In each case Marcel introduced me, and I showed them my badge and ID. I then explained that a second guest had died during the night and that because both deaths had occurred suddenly and unexpectedly, the coroner's office would have to be notified and might want to send someone up when the roads were cleared. So, as a matter of routine, we had to ask everyone a few questions while their memories were fresh, and then the results would be passed on to the Office of the Chief Medical Examiner.

I won't go through it all here. You can probably imagine the span of questions we asked each person, like had they seen or heard anyone or anything at all unusual in or around the resort on either of the previous two days or evenings? Also, in the context of what they may have heard or seen, I asked about each person's movements on those days.

The responses involved a lot of questions about what constitutes 'unusual' and a lot of responses along the lines of no, they hadn't noticed anything. My careful questioning about people's activities didn't turn up anything. It seemed that hardly anyone would have had alibies for the night of Gary's death in particular, which wouldn't have been unusual and, in any case, I was careful not to push that angle for fear of any suggestion that the death may not have been accidental.

I did learn one interesting thing from these interviews. Three of the staff had each taken a shift at the front desk over the previous 24 hours. The evening staff member, who had worked from 4 pm to midnight, remembered seeing a few people – almost all staff members - come to the front, pull boots on, and then go out for walks or simply to stand outside for a smoke, but that this happened so frequently, and the staff members were so familiar to him, that he took no particular notice. He did remember seeing Gary go out though.

"Big fellow, always wearing a lumberjack shirt," he said. "I remember seeing him go out, partly because of the shirt he always wore and partly because he seemed under-dressed for the weather. He might have had a jacket with him, but if so, he wasn't wearing it and I didn't see it. I remembered that he had been helping Kevin with the generator though, so I just assumed that was where he was going, and that he was lightly dressed because the generator shed is so close, and because it's so hot in there when both generators are running."

"When did you see him go out?"

"Just after ten o'clock."

"Did you see him again after that?" I asked.

"No. If he came back, it must have been after my shift changed at midnight."

The 'graveyard-shift' staff member, who had worked from midnight to 8 am, also remembered seeing a few people come to the front and go outside to smoke. Again, it appeared that this was a common occurrence. This staff member also thought he remembered seeing Gary go out.

"He's the guy with the bright red jacket," he said. "I think he must have gone out for a smoke. Lots of skiers do that – have one last smoke, I mean - before turning in for the night."

"When did you see him go out?"

"Just after I came on shift. Probably about 1 am I think, I didn't really pay much attention."

"Did you see him again after that?" I asked.

"No. I might not have looked up at the right time, or I might have been in the back office catching up on paperwork. I don't actually sit at the front desk itself much on that shift because there's so little going on and there is a bell people can ring if they need me to come to the desk."

Everyone seemed to have heard something about either or both deaths, and the stories that were circulating among the staff seemed to refer to an injured woman that hadn't come out of a coma and a male guest that had been overcome by fumes while trying to refuel the generators.

Those explanations were true enough, as far as they went, and I tried not to disillusion anyone, simply repeating that we were going through the routine to assist the coroner's office, which was also true, as far as it went.

We weren't able to speak to Kevin or Gerry, of course, since they had gone off on the snowmobiles. Gerry's absence, however, explained why no one had missed Gary during the night: Dianne had already said goodnight to him and gone to the suite she shared with Pat, so Gerry and Gary's suite had remained empty that night. Consistent with this, one of the housekeepers confirmed that neither of the beds had been slept in on the night Gary died.

Finally, we called in each of Barry, Dianne, Pat, and Kate individually, but didn't learn much from any of them.

Barry hadn't heard or noticed anything at all. Explaining that I had to prepare a report on both days, I carefully asked him a few questions about Tuesday, the day that Sandra had died. He said that he'd been by her bedside virtually all day.

"Virtually?" I asked.

"Well, I had to leave her room go to the bathroom occasionally of course, and I did leave the suite itself for a few minutes."

"When was that?"

"Sometime in the middle of the afternoon. Just after you were in to visit, in fact."

"OK, and where did you go?"

"To see the manager, Marcel. It was strange too because Marcel had asked to see me about something, but then I couldn't find him." Seeing my look of confusion, he elaborated further: "Sorry, I'm not explaining this very well. Just after lunch, I found a note pushed under the main door of our suite. It was on resort stationery, and it asked if I would please go and see the manager, in his office, about the credit card they had put on file for our stay. It specifically asked if I could be there at a specific time. I think it was 3 pm. When I got to the manager's office Marcel wasn't there. The staff member at the front desk didn't know where he was, so I decided to wait for a few minutes. I really wanted to be with Sandra though, so I eventually gave up and went back, but when I got there..." He put his head in his hands and shuddered. Taking a deep breath, he continued. "When I got there, I immediately went to check on her and, well, you know the rest."

"Yes, I see. It's not your fault, you know."

"Dianne hadn't really expected her to come out of the coma. It's just that I tried so hard to be there with her - for her - at the end, but I wasn't. It's horrible thinking that she died all alone."

"I'm sure she wasn't conscious, so she wouldn't have known anything and she wouldn't have felt any pain or anything like that."

"No. I hope not, anyway."

"So, just for my report then, how long would you say you were gone from the room?"

"I don't know," he said, consideringly. "Let's say five minutes to walk to the manager's office; maybe 15 minutes waiting for him; then another five minutes to walk back to our rooms. That would make it something like 30 minutes, give or take?"

"Thank you. Would anyone else have been able to go visit Sandra while you were away?"

"Sure. When I left the suite, I left the main door unlocked for that exact reason: because so many people had been dropping in to check on Sandra's condition."

That was about all I got from Barry, so I thanked him and moved on to track down Dianne.

When I did, all I got from her was that she couldn't recall anything she hadn't already told us previously.

"It feels like everyone around me is suddenly dying," said Dianne. "First my sister and now Gary."

"I'm very sorry," I said, not for the first time. As Dianne got up to leave, I let her get to the door before saying, "One last question. In your professional opinion, was Gary likely to have wanted to commit suicide?"

"Absolutely not!" she exclaimed. "The idea's absurd." And with that, she left, slamming the door behind her.

"You got under her skin there," said Marcel.

"Yes. I think that's the first time I've seen her show any real emotion since we got up here. I wonder why," and, in my inner voice, I thought, *I wonder if it was real?*

When it was Pat's turn, she said she'd spent a quiet night. "At one point I went to the kitchen, which was deserted, raided the fridges and then snuck back to my room with my snack. After that I went to bed and slept through the night."

"OK, thanks. By the way, how are Barry and Dianne doing?"

"Pretty well, I think. They're spending a lot of time together. Consoling each other, I guess."

"You told me once that they used to be a couple?"

"Yes. Barry broke up with her so he could take up with Sandra, and I'm not sure Dianne ever really got over it. They seem so glued to each other now, that I've been wondering whether they'll get back together now. We'll see, I guess."

Last, but not least, was Kate. Like Pat, she said that she'd had a quiet night, watched a TV movie in her room before turning in to get some sleep, and had neither seen nor heard anything unusual. When I thanked her, she got up and walked to the door. I waited until she'd opened the door and was half-way through before asking my last question.

"By the way Kate, you're not a smoker are you?"

Since she'd turned her head back towards me, I was able to watch her expression. She froze. It was only for an instant, but for that one fleeting instant her whole body froze. I could imagine the wheels, furiously turning in her mind, but all she said was "No, I'm not. Why do you ask?"

"Just curious," I replied. "Apparently there were a few people popping out the front door to smoke from time to time, and if you were one of those, I wondered whether you might have seen or heard anything unusual." This was the truth, but not the whole truth.

"Well, I suppose I might have if I'd gone out, but I didn't. Anything else?"

"No. Thanks again," I replied.

After Kate and Marcel had left, I was alone in the conference room organizing my notes when there was a knock on the door. It was Renée, one of the housekeepers. I had questioned her about an hour before.

"Excuse me, miss," she said, "but you said you wanted to know about anything unusual we might have seen in the last few days?"

"Yes, that's right," I confirmed, "please come in and sit down."

Taking a chair, she hesitated. "It's just a little thing, but you said anything unusual no matter how small?"

"Yes, that's quite correct. Have you remembered something?"

"Well yes. This week it has been my turn to make up the rooms along the corridor that you are staying in. That also includes the family suite that Miss Sandra Hayward was staying in."

"The one that's right next to the suite I'm in."

"Yes. Well, the thing I noticed was that Miss Hayward seemed to be losing her hair."

"What do you mean, losing?"

"Well, every morning when I made up her bed, I noticed that there would be quite a few hairs left on her pillow. Individual hairs, not clumps of hairs, as if they'd fallen out rather than been pulled out, if you know what I mean."

I nodded. "Don't you usually find that people lose a few hairs at night and leave them on their pillows?"

"Oh, yes. For sure. Especially people with long hair. But there was more than I've ever seen before. Most people wouldn't even notice, I'm sure, since her hair was blonde and fairly short. But there was quite a lot, and it was very noticeable on her pillow each morning."

"How many days did you notice this hair loss?" I asked.

"Everyday! What I mean is, that there were hairs on her pillow every morning when I went to make-up the room... even after they'd taken her body away."

"Interesting. OK. Thank you for letting me know."

As she got up to leave, I went back to organizing my notes. When I looked up again, I saw that she had stopped at the door and was clearly hesitating."

"Was there something else?" I asked, as neutrally as I could.

She just stood there for a moment, by the door, then seemed to come to a decision and came back and sat down again. "There is one more thing. I don't suppose it's important, and it doesn't make me look very good, but you did say to tell you about anything unusual." It was half statement, half question, and the look in her eyes was questioning.

"Yes. Anything at all. Sometimes the smallest detail can be important. Sometimes not, of course. We often don't know what's important and what isn't until we've looked at everything and heard from everybody... What else have you remembered?"

"It's about Miss Hayward's room again. This morning, when I cleaned and made up her room – she, her body that is, was gone by then of course – there was another strange thing besides the hairs on the pillow. When I went to dump out the waste basket by her bed, there was quite a 'thump' as something heavy fell out. It seemed a little odd, so I reached into the garbage to find out what it was. Sometimes, you see, people accidentally drop a watch or a water glass or something into the waste basket, so I like to check to be sure. In this case, I thought from the sound that it was heavier, like a travel clock, for example. I've found several of those accidentally knocked in to the waste basket, and the guests have been quite thankful to have them rescued. You see?"

"Yes, I can imagine. Is that what it was in this case?"

"No. It was a jar of face cream. The jar and label were very fancy and expensive looking, and the price label was still on the bottom. It had been very expensive!"

I frowned. "Is that unusual? To find old cosmetic containers in the trash I mean?"

"Oh. No. Not at all. Not when they're used up anyway. But that's what caught my attention in this case. It was so heavy it didn't feel right. That's why I opened it. I was surprised to find that it was nearly full. It must have only been used a couple of times since it was new."

"Nearly full. Hmmm. Maybe she tried it and didn't like it. Oh, well, thank you for telling me, I'll make a note of it."

Renée got up and walked to the door. She was just reaching for the door handle, when I thought of another question.

"I suppose it's gone now?"

"Gone?" she asked, turning to face me.

"The face cream jar. It's gone out with the trash?"

Renée's face turned beet-red. "Not exactly. You see, I kept it for myself. It's not really stealing is it, if I find something in the trash I mean?"

"Not if it was purposely thrown out, no. Do you still have it then?"

She nodded.

"Would you mind bringing it here so I can take a look at it then?"

"Sure," she said, sounding relieved, and she left to fetch it.

When she arrived back, a few minutes later, she brought in a nearly full jar made of pearlescent-white glass, with a stylish gold top. I held it by the edges and unscrewed the top. Inside was a thick-looking white cream. The label on the front had a 19th century apothecary look to it, with a manufacturer's name I'd never heard of, and the product itself identified as 𝕮𝖗𝖊𝖒𝖆 𝖉𝖊 𝕭𝖊𝖑𝖑𝖊𝖟𝖆.

"I don't suppose you know any Spanish?" I asked.

"I know some. That's another reason the jar attracted me. I'm studying South American history in university. Crema de belleza means beauty cream."

"Can you translate the rest of the front label too?"

"Well, it says *Aclaramiento de piel. Elimina líneas de expresión, manchas de sol, paño, y acne.* That means, *Skin lightening. Eliminates fine lines, sun spots, dark spots, and acne.*"

"Skin lightening," I repeated. Turning the jar upside down, I read the price label. "Five-hundred dollars! Who pays $500 for a jar of beauty cream? U.S. dollars too, I'll bet."

"Not me," smiled Renée.

"Not me either," I agreed. Then I turned the jar again and scanned the label on the back.

"Renée, I'd like to keep this for a while. OK? I'll give you a receipt for it and you'll get it back later."

She agreed, and I wrote her out a receipt.

"Anything else your sharp eyes have noticed?" I asked with a smile.

"I don't think so."

"Well, thank you for telling me everything, and for showing me this."

"You're welcome," she said, and left looking relieved. *Probably relieved she's won't get into trouble for keeping the cosmetic jar,* I thought, as I continued to look at it. But my mind wasn't on Renée anymore.

When I had my notes assembled, I left the conference room and went to ask Marcel where he was going to store the body.

"In one of the unheated storage sheds outside, near the generator shack. That's where we put the young woman's body as well."

The rest of the day was unremarkable. The lunchtime crowd consisted of only Pat, Don, and I so we naturally invited Pat to sit with us.

"It's so quiet here now," began Pat when she sat down.

"Have you seen Barry or Dianne?" I asked.

"Oh, yes. They're still glued together. Consoling each other, I suppose, but I think it's gone a bit further than that already. They're having lunch in Barry's suite, and this morning Dianne moved out of her bedroom in my suite and into his."

"And you disapprove?"

"Oh, no. Not really. If they can help each other, then that's a good thing…" she paused for a moment.

"But?" I prompted.

"I don't know, something about it seems wrong to me. Maybe I'm just being catty, or maybe it's just that I'm missing Gerry. He should have been back by now, and I'm getting worried."

"I'm sure they're OK," put in Don. "Even if one of the snowmobiles broke down, they'd have been able to double-up on the other one and still make it into Banff. If they don't get back by tonight, then I'm sure they'll have found a way to return by tomorrow."

"I hope so," said Pat, with a tremor.

Since there wasn't much else we could do for her, we changed the subject to lighter topics, which helped us get through lunch together.

Suppertime, when it came, was almost a replay of lunch, except that Barry and Dianne did make an appearance but selected a table for two. When Pat walked in, she was presented with the choice of either trying to get the couple to move to a large table or joining Don and I. She chose the latter.

"See what I mean?" she said, as she took her seat with us. "Like two peas in a pod."

"Everyone deals with grief in their own way, Pat," I offered. "I'm sure they'll unwind and open up eventually. You just have to give them time."

"I suppose," she said, with a sigh. "And no sign of our errant snowmobilers yet either. I just checked with the manager. He hasn't seen any sign of them yet either."

"Did he seem worried?" asked Don.

"No. Not at all. In fact, he seems to think like you do, that they probably had some kind of mechanical problem and will probably show up tomorrow. Seems like kind of an optimist to me."

That made Don smile. "You mean a pessimist about the snowmobiles and an optimist about getting back tomorrow?"

"All right, I'm not being very logical, am I?" said Pat, ruefully. "Some scientist I'm going to make."

"Scientists are human too," I put in. "Your concerns are very natural. We're just trying to help you not worry too much."

"Thanks. Part of the problem is that, being so cut-off and isolated up here, there isn't much else to do but think and worry."

I must admit that Pat had a point. Later that evening, I myself fell into a contemplative mood.

I'd been sitting in front of the fireplace in our shared living room. The natural gas fire was dancing and burning brightly, and I'd just gotten up to make myself a mug of hot chocolate.

When I returned to the comfortable armchair in front of the fire, I picked up Sandra's jar of facial cream that I'd been contemplating and stared into the dancing flames again. The longer I did so, images from the previous two days began to appear in my mind, and they seemed to go backwards in time, changing in synch with the sounds of the fire.

'Pop'   *Gary, lying stretched-out on the floor beside one of the generators.*

'Pop'   *Sandra, lying dead in her bed.*

'Snap'   *Sandra, lying crumpled-up, at the bottom of the chute.*

'Crackle' *Sandra, who had struggled so much to get on the chair lift.*

Lost in thought, I was only vaguely aware of Don coming into the room and sitting down in the armchair on the other side of the fireplace.

"Thinking or dozing?" he asked.

"Hmm? Yes… No…" then I surfaced. "Both, I guess."

He waited, giving me time to get my thoughts in order. Then, I looked up at him. "Don, I think I know at least part of what's been going on…"

"OK. Want to try a theory out on me?"

"Yes. Let's begin with Sandra. When we went for that short hike the first afternoon we were here, do you remember how fragile and uncoordinated she seemed to be? Especially when she tried to get on and off the chairlift?"

"I sure do. I wondered whether she might be suffering from a Vitamin E deficiency, or possibly MS[15], or that maybe she just wasn't much of an outdoors person and had never been to a ski hill before."

"It was that last one for me. I actually thought she'd maybe never seen a chair lift before, and she seemed so timid that I thought it was mostly that she tended to hesitate at the wrong times. So, she'd step back when she really needed to step up and onto the chair, or to freeze when she needed to slide to the edge and then step down and off the chair to get off. I remember you saying that she probably just needed more practice."

"Right."

"OK, fast-forward to the next day when we did our scramble to the summit of the mountain. When we came back, we were just in time to hear the scream and backtrack to where the three couples had been trying some rock climbing. They'd somehow talked Sandra into trying to overcome her timidity and attempt to climb the rock wall, but again she wasn't able to pull it off and took that big fall."

"Yes. I remember thinking that the wall they had been climbing looked like a good choice for beginners, because it had so many nice hand- and footholds to choose from. It should have been almost as easy as climbing a ladder," said Don.

"Right. So, once again I put it down to a combination of her being quite timid, not very coordinated, and again trying an activity for the first time."

"OK, so we have two instances of that now."

"Yes. Now let's move ahead to the next morning. After I had dropped by to see how she was doing, I was walking down the hallway with Kate and noticed that she was trying to shake something off of her fingers. It was hair. Sandra's hair. Kate said that there had been hairs lying on the pillow, on each side of her head. She said she thought that they must have become dislodged when she hit her head, and I didn't question her, but it didn't seem like a very probably explanation to me. Hairs usually either fall out or get pulled out, and when they're pulled out, they tend to come away in clumps. Kate mentioned individual hairs."

"So?"

"Well, something about hair falling out seemed familiar to me but at the time, I couldn't remember why, so I let the thought go."

"But now you've remembered?" Don prompted.

"I have," I nodded. "It came back to me this afternoon, when I was interviewing the staff about anything they'd seen or heard over the previous two days. One of the housekeepers, a woman named Renée, said she'd noticed that Sandra seemed to be losing her hair. When I questioned her further, she said that she found hairs left on Sandra's pillow every morning when she went in to makeup her room – including the first morning, which was before Sandra had her accident on the rock wall."

"OK, so it wasn't due to the accident. Some kind of medical condition then?"

"Yes, and I think I know what it was. Renée eventually admitted to me that she found a nearly full jar of expensive facial cream in the trash basket of Sandra's room. This was after the body had been removed and Renée was cleaning the whole room. She was embarrassed to admit to it because she'd taken it for herself, since it seemed so expensive and so nearly new."

"And it had been thrown away."

"Yes, but I imagine the staff aren't supposed to keep anything expensive that they find, in case it was a mistake and the owners should come back looking for it. Anyway, I asked her to show it to me. Here it is." I picked up the jar from the side-table beside my chair, and handed it over. I'd put it in a clear plastic bag.

"Crema de Belleza," read Don. "Some kind of facial cream you say?"

"Yes. It's for lightening the skin, so darker pigments and blemishes don't show as much. That kind of thing."

"OK. So, what's the big deal?"

"Read the other label."

Don turned the jar over, then whistled. "Holy smokes! Five-hundred dollars. That's crazy."

"Yes. That too, but I meant the other label."

This time Don looked at the label on the back of the jar. "It's in

79

Spanish, but the upper part looks like instructions for use, and the bottom is the ingredients. Right?"

"Right. The ingredient that caught my eye is calomel."

"What's that?"

"The term comes from ancient Greek and seems to be the same in English or Spanish – it means mercurous chloride."

"Isn't mercury poisonous?"

"Yes. That's why it's illegal to sell products like this in Canada[16]. If you were to rub this stuff on your face every day, you would get a bit of mercury into your system by inhaling the vapour released from the cream, and you'd get even more from the contact between the cream and your skin. Over time, it would accumulate in your body. If you kept at it, you would eventually show the symptoms of mercury poisoning."

"Which are?"

"Anxiety, dizziness, mood changes, tremors, muscle weakness, lack of motor skills… the list goes on. One of the symptoms of reaching toxic levels is hair loss. You may have read about people with thallium poisoning experiencing hair loss? The same goes for mercury."

"How do you know all this?"

"When I was a chemistry student in university, one of our professors was frequently quite jumpy. By that I mean both mentally and physically. He tended to be anxious, irritable, and his moods could change quickly. As time went on, we noticed that he seemed to have difficulty remembering things, and he had what some people unkindly called 'the shakes.' He was a smoker, and he always seemed to have trouble lighting his pipe because both hands would be shaking.

"We were chemistry students, not medical students, but we eventually became convinced that he had Mad Hatters' Disease[17] - mercury poisoning. He certainly displayed almost all the classic symptoms."

"Where would he have been exposed to mercury? Fish?"

"No, not fish, that would have been methylmercury poisoning. I mean poisoning from metallic mercury. His specialty was physical chemistry and his laboratory was full of apparatus that used mercury to change the pressure and volume conditions of the chemical reactions he was studying. He had several complicated arrangements of interconnected glass vessels and tubing, and by pumping mercury in or out he could easily change the effective internal volume and, if the apparatus was sealed, also the pressure. That actually took a lot of mercury, and he was often seen in his lab moving mercury around, cleaning it., and so on. He wasn't very careful about it either, and he splashed and spilled so much of it that we students became afraid to even go into his lab."

"What happened to him?"

"He died a few years after I graduated. I've always suspected that it was the mercury that killed him."

"So, you think Sandra was using this cream with the mercury in it, and it built-up in her system until she showed the symptoms that we both noticed?"

"Right."

"And that either caused or contributed to her falling off the chair lift and falling off the rock wall?"

"Right."

"And killed her?"

"Maybe. It could have contributed to her coma, or even caused it but it's pretty rare for people to die from using these skin creams. I was wondering whether someone might have been helping it along by boosting the mercury content."

"Sneaky," said Don. "You mean that if someone wanted to poison her, they could add extra mercury to the cream, give it to her, and then when she dies mercury would show up from the post-mortem, but people would think that it was from a bad batch of face cream."

"Yes."

"Then why throw away the jar?"

"I don't know. Maybe it can be traced to the purchaser."

"You're going to have the jar fingerprinted then. That's why it's in a bag?"

"Yes, but I'd doubt we'll find much. If I'm right about the mercury, and the reason for throwing away the jar, then it will have been wiped clean before it was tossed in the trash. In that case, it'll only have Renée's prints on it."

"Who would have access to mercury?"

"Well, I suppose you could buy a bunch of old-style mercury thermometers and remove the mercury from them. Some kinds of technical and professional people would be able to get it from their workplaces."

"Would that apply to any of the people up here?"
"I was thinking about that:

- o Dianne Hayward is a medical resident. She would have access to the hospital's labs and its pharmacy, which would allow her to get at mercury manometers and thermometers, not to mention other mercury-containing products,
- o Barry Hawkins is a graduate student in chemistry, he'd have access to the metal mercury and also to a wide range of mercury compounds,
- o Gary Parks was a graduate student in mineral process engineering, and the standard processes for extracting gold and silver from their ores involves the use of mercury, so their labs would have it in stock even if he was actually doing research in something else,
- o Pat Lansing is a student in petroleum geology, and would certainly be familiar with a rock characterization technique called mercury porosimetry,
- o Gerry Gilbert is a physics student, and on the first day we met he told us about his research on gas pressures, which involves using mercury manometers, and
- o Kate Morrison is a dentistry student. Dentists mix a powdered alloy with mercury metal to form an amalgam putty that is used to fill cavities in teeth. I have some of those fillings myself, in a couple of my back molars.

"Any or all of them should know about the hazards of mercury poisoning, and each of them would have had access to mercury – either as the pure metal or as an inorganic salt."

"If it's hazardous, wouldn't it have ben carefully inventoried and locked up?" asked Don.

"No. The only chemicals that are normally locked up are the really expensive ones, regulated drugs, and ethanol of course – to keep the students from drinking it. Any laboratory that uses a lot of mercury wouldn't keep a close inventory, and wouldn't be likely to notice if someone stole a small amount. For someone of Sandra's size, a lethal dose would be something like ten grams, maybe less."

"So. They're all suspects then. At least, all of the ones that are still alive."

"Yes. Barry, Dianne, Pat, Gerry, and Kate. Sandra was a psychology student, so even if she had read the ingredients label on the back of the facial cream jar, she wouldn't necessarily know what the word calomel means. So, she might not have had any idea that the cream she was using was hazardous."

"How about the resort staff?"

"Possible, but unlikely don't you think? There aren't many staff up here right now, and there were just us eight guests staying overnight. The odds of any of the staff knowing any of the guests, much less having a grudge against any of us seems pretty improbable. I agree we should try to keep our minds open though."

"OK, but how did Sandra actually die? You think that the mercury in her system combined in some bad way with the effects of the fall from the rock face?"

"It's possible, I suppose. I don't know anything about the mechanics of a coma or what chemical interactions might make a coma worse. I was thinking of a simpler solution. Suppose someone was trying to kill Sandra in a slow, methodical way that might ultimately appear natural, but if an autopsy was conducted would show mercury in her system. An investigation might find the cosmetic jar, in which case the authorities would probably conclude that she'd been accidentally poisoned by a dangerous product that shouldn't have been allowed into the country in the first place."

"Right."

"OK then. Now suppose the poisoner is up here on the mountain with us. They see her take the fall. Maybe they were even one of the ones encouraging her to try a climb that was beyond her abilities, or maybe they kept well in the background. In any case, they see her go in to a coma and what do they think? Well, number one would be maybe this will solve their problem and finish her off, right? So, they sit back and patiently watch. But then, things change and Sandra is beginning to get better, so maybe she'll recover after all. But at that moment she's still unable to move her body. Her poisoner sees an opportunity, waits until she is alone, and goes in and shuts off her breathing."

"I suppose that would work. All a person would have to do is recognize the opportunity, get some time alone with Sandra, be quick and then get out. But wasn't Barry pretty much glued to her bedside the whole time?"

"That's what I thought until I interviewed him today. Aside from brief spells like going to the bathroom and so on, there was one time where he left the entire suite to go meet with Marcel. He estimates that he was gone from the room for about half an hour."

"That would have been more than enough if your mystery person was waiting and watching, and if they had the nerve to go through with it."

"Yes, and get this. The reason Barry went to meet Marcel was because of a note that had been pushed under their door, but when he got to the Front Desk…"

"No Marcel."

"Right. I'll check with Marcel in the morning, but I'll bet you he never sent any note."

"Do you have the note?"

"No. I didn't want to push Barry with too many questions when we were mostly supposed to be talking about the circumstances of Gary's death, but I can still ask about it later."

Don had more thoughts to offer. "OK then. Let's say you've got the story about right so far. Now, if Gary was killed by the same person that killed Sandra, then we can cross off Gerry as a suspect, because he went down the mountain with Kevin before Gary was killed."

"Yes. As long as he really went down the mountain, and didn't sneak back."

"Riiight," said Don thoughtfully. "You do have a devious mind, don't you?"

"So I've been told. It does complicate things for me."

"But it's partly why you're so good at your job. I would have been inclined to eliminate Pat and Gerry as suspects, and focus on Barry, Dianne, and Kate."

"Well, Silver might agree with you there. He's usually very sensitive to people, and sometimes their emotions and even their thoughts. Have you noticed that he really liked Sandra, was pretty neutral about almost everyone else, but seemed to take a dislike to Barry, Dianne, and Kate?"

'No, I guess I didn't," replied Don, "you think it means something?"

"Hard to say. He didn't react to any of them as strongly as he has to some of the worst villains we've encountered in our time, and his reasons might not have anything to do with the murders.

Remember, how we brushed off his reaction to Kate as probably being due to the Siamese cat smells on her clothing?"

"OK. So, nothing conclusive on that front then, but I still think that Barry, for example, might have wanted to get away from Sandra without having to break-up with Dianne's baby sister."

"I suppose," I offered, "although he doesn't seem like someone that has difficulty getting out of relationships. Just ask Dianne or Kate."

"OK then, how about Dianne or Kate? As former girlfriends, either might have wanted to get Sandra out of the way and make a play to reunite with Barry. In Dianne's case that could be a motive for polishing-off Gary too."

"Doesn't seem like a reason to murder someone, but who knows, we may get there yet. We'll have to see."

It started snowing again that night.

Laurie Schramm

7 MORE TROUBLE

Later that night - well past midnight - Pat, who had also been lounging in front of the natural gas fireplace in the family room of her and Dianne's suite, had fallen into a doze. Some time later, she transitioned into a deep sleep.

Not long after this, a shadowy figure approached the room from the outside. Being unlocked, the sliding door opened easily, and it slid fully open quite quietly. The figure entered and checked to make sure Pat was asleep. Satisfied that she was, the figure then closed the doors to both bedrooms, closed the fireplace flue-damper, pushed rugs up at the base of the doors to the hallway and both bedrooms, jamming them up to block the entry of fresh air, then left.

Day 7: Thursday, October 25, 1979

The famous American baseball player Yogi Berra is reported to have once said: "It's *déjà vu* all over again." That's how I felt the next morning, as we again woke up to the sound of someone loudly knocking on the door to our suite. Once again, it was Marcel and, once again, it was trouble.

"I'm very sorry to disturb you, but there's been another incident."

"Another one!" I exclaimed, but I pulled some clothes on, asked Don to look after Silver, and then followed Marcel. I was surprised that this time he had only to lead me to the next suite: that of Pat and Dianne.

There in the family room, I saw Pat lying on the ground coughing, with Dianne hovering over her.

Marcel led me over to a very pale-looking Renée, who was sitting on a couch to one side. "Tell her what happened," he said.

"I was doing the rooms in this section and had knocked on the door to see if I could go in and make up the room for the day. There was no response, and the deadbolt had not been set, so I unlocked the door and walked in. When I did, I found Miss Lansing sitting in one of the big chairs in front of the fireplace. At first, I thought she was asleep but she didn't look right: her face was all red. Then I noticed that the air didn't smell right either.

"For some reason, I thought to look at the fireplace. It was turned on, but the flue-damper was in the closed position so I opened the damper and turned off the fireplace. I threw the hallway door wide open and ran over and opened the big sliding glass door. Then, I tried to wake her up but she didn't seem to be breathing so I tilted her head back and gave her artificial respiration: five or six cycles of mouth-to-mouth. Then I stopped to see if she had a pulse. She did, but it was very weak. I gave her one more big breath, then grabbed the phone and called the Front Desk. They called Dr. Hayward" – she pointed towards Dianne - who arrived a few minutes later and took over.

"Thank you, Renée. That was a very clear summary," I said, then went over and put my hand on Dianne's shoulder.

"How is she?" I asked.

"Not bad, but it was a close call. Her breathing is steady and her normal colour is coming back."

"What was that about her looking all red in the face?"

"I think I explained this before. Red skin colouring is an indicator of carbon monoxide poisoning. The pronounced red colour comes with elevated, usually fatal, levels of carboxyhemoglobin in the blood. That's what I mean about it being a close call. Pat might have been dead in another hour or two."

As she was speaking, I'd noticed that Dianne herself was looking very pale.

"Are you OK Dianne?"

"Yes, I'm fine. But I can't help feeling like this was my fault. I'd moved over to Sandra's old room yesterday, so I could spend more time with Barry. If I'd stayed here instead, I might have noticed that the flue-damper was closed, or at least I would have woken Pat up to go to bed, in which case one of us would have turned the fireplace off. She's done that before, dozed off sitting by the fire I mean, and on the other nights I had to rouse her to go to bed when I did."

Just then, Barry came in and rushed over to Dianne to ask what had happened.

"Carbon monoxide from the fireplace. It was a close call, but Pat will be OK now," she said.

"Has anything else in the room been touched?" I asked Marcel.

"Not as far as I know," he replied.

"Fine. Give me a few minutes to look around, then I'll come and find you."

"I'll be in my office," he replied then promptly left, presumably relieved to be able to get away from the sight of the body.

An examination of the fireplace showed that the flue-damper was now open position, and there was a highly visible sign posted nearby warning guests to always keep the flue-damper open. I sighed. Pat had struck me as very outdoorsy and competent; the kind of person that would be knowledgeable about fires and fireplaces, and careful enough not to forget to open the flue-damper before lighting a fire in a fireplace.

Because of this, I wasn't shocked to see two sets of footprints in the fresh snow outside the room's sliding glass door. One set led to the door, while another set led away from it. Just inside the door, and to one side, there was a small region of the carpet, oval-shaped and perhaps one foot by two feet, that was very wet. *Hmmm*, I thought.

The only other things that seemed out of place in the room were the area rugs. One was bunched up by the door to Pat's bedroom, while another one was bunched up by the door to Dianne's bedroom. When I shifted them and opened the bedroom doors everything looked like one would expect following the previously day's room cleaning. In both rooms, the beds were made and appeared undisturbed, and the windows were locked closed.

Over by the main door to the family room, the one Marcel and I had entered through, was a third rug, the one that normally lay by the sliding glass door. This was also bunched up but pushed to one side.

If there were any other clues present in the suite, I didn't spot them. Taking my leave, I went back to Don's and my suite to get Silver, my camera, and a jacket. I gave him a brief summary of what had happened and finished by saying that I was planning to go outside for a closer look at the footprints.

"Want some company?" asked Don.

"Sure. It will also save me from having to repeat everything to you later."

When we reached the front lobby, we not only went for our boots but I looked at every other pair of shoes and boots in the racks by the front doors.

"What are you looking for?" asked Don.

"Anything in size 13… Ah ha! Look what we have here!" I held up a large hiking boot. "Men's size 13."

"Wait a minute," said Don. "When we looked at all of the boots and shoes that were here yesterday morning, there was nothing in size 13."

"That's right. I bet that when we go ask Dianne, she'll tell us that Gary brought two pairs of boots up here with him. These hiking boots, which he would have worn for his hikes in the meadows and over to the rock wall they were climbing, and also the big felt-pack boots in case we got a big dump of snow. Let's go check the tracks."

Taking one of the hiking boots with me, we went out the front door and just far enough to be sure we were looking at the trail to Pat's suite, but not so far that anyone looking out from the suite would have been able to see us.

Crouching down beside a clear-looking boot-print, I compared it with the one in my hand. One looked like the mirror-image of the other. Then I tried placing the boot in one of the prints.

"Seems to fit perfectly," I remarked.

"You don't sound surprised," said Don.

"I'm not, really. It would have been so easy for anyone to steal Gary's boots, wear them here, go in and see that Pat had fallen asleep, set her up to die, and then walk back to the front entrance and put them back on the rack."

"Essentially the same trick that someone pulled with Gary's other boots at the generator shack," said Don, nodding his head.

"And we already established that there isn't anyone else up here with feet as large as Gary's. So, it really could have been anyone but it was probably our mystery person."

"Right." Selecting an untouched boot-print in the snow, I placed the boot beside it, but lying on its side, then took pictures of the two together and of each individually.

When I stood up. I looked around but didn't see anything lying on the snow. "I'll ask Dianne whether they kept the sliding glass door locked at night, but I have a feeling that the answer will be no."

"That would be weird under normal circumstances, but with so few people up here right now most people wouldn't think there was much risk of an intruder trying to break in," observed Don.

"We locked ours every night," I countered.

"Just shows what suspicious people we've become," said Don, with a smile.

"If their living room curtains were open, like they are now, anyone would be able to look in from the outside and see that someone was sitting in front of the fire. You could even guess from the person's size, width of shoulders, and blonde hair that it was Pat. But how would you know if she was awake or asleep? And very few people would know that Dianne wasn't in the adjoining bedroom."

"It would have meant taking a risk, but at two or three o'clock in the morning, say, and with all of us being extra tired from being at this altitude, chances are they'd both be asleep even if Dianne was there too," said Don. "And the intruder might have simply stood here and tried knocking on the door first, just to be sure."

"I suppose. It's true that we're all feeling the effects of the altitude. It still brings us back to the same small pool of suspects though."

I took a look at Silver who was sitting patiently beside me, looking around. "Doesn't look like anything out here has attracted Silver's attention. Why don't we go back inside? I think we've learned as much as we can out here."

When we reached the front of the hotel, Don took Silver off while I went to find Marcel. The first thing I did was to ask him to store Gary's hiking boots somewhere safe for me. The second thing was to ask to speak with the staff that would have been on Front Desk duty during the night.

The staff member that had been on the 4 pm to midnight shift had apparently not noticed anything, and had so little to offer that I strongly suspected that they had been reading or sleeping, or otherwise ignoring their duty altogether.

In contrast, the young man who had the midnight to 8 am shift seemed to have noticed everything. I was willing to wait, but Marcel insisted in waking him up and, although he was a bit drowsy from only having had a few hours sleep, he was pleasant enough about it and his memory seemed clear.

"There were only a few people up and around at that time of night," he explained. "Almost all of them were other staff members going outside to smoke."

It never ceased to amaze me how many otherwise active and healthy-looking ski people were also smokers. Just one of life's contradictions, I suppose. Anyway, the desk clerk had only seen one non-staff person go by.

"There was that one guest, the one that looks like a lumberjack. Anyway, he was wearing his bright red jacket, so there was no missing him. We all know that he'd been helping Kevin with the generator, so I figured that was where he was going."

It never fails, I thought. *You try to interview everyone that might know something useful, but....* This man hadn't been interviewed yesterday because he was sound asleep after working the 'graveyard shift.' So, he didn't know that Gary was dead. "Did you get a look at the person's face or hair?" I asked.

"No, I only saw him from the back, and he had his hood up."

"What time was this?"

"I didn't pay any attention to the time. Might have been around 2 am, maybe later than that."

"OK then, did you see him come back later?"

"No, but then I wasn't sitting at the desk every minute. Sometimes I had to go into the office for things related to the paperwork I was doing, or for coffee. You drink a lot of coffee at 3 and 4 in the morning if you want to stay awake. Or to go to the bathroom of course, which happens a few times because of all that coffee." He smiled.

"Right. Well, thank you," I said.

I didn't ask to interview all the staff again this time, but I did ask Marcel if I could speak to whomever it was that did the general maintenance and repair for the resort. Marcel had replied that they had three such people, but that only one of them – a young man named George - was present at the resort, the other two having been stranded in Banff by the snowstorm.

George the handyman, as the staff called him, was easily the oldest of the staff at the resort and had a very relaxed, almost vague manner. However, there was nothing vague about his responses when I asked him about anything to do with his duties. His eyes brightened, and he was very clear and credible in his assertion that all of the natural gas fireplaces were in good working order, and had all been inspected before the resort had opened for the pre-skiing season. He even outlined the inspection steps he had taken with each and every fireplace. That had been about three weeks before we arrived. He also pointed out that it was resort policy that, when the rooms were occupied, the housekeepers were required to make sure that the flue-dampers were in the open position every day when they went in to make up the rooms. The reason, he explained, was that despite the clear signs on each fireplace there were always a few guests who didn't bother to read the signs and didn't think to open the flue-dampers. It was only when the rooms were unoccupied that the flue-dampers were closed, to save on heating costs.

When I went back to Pat's suite to check on her condition – which was steadily improving – I was pleased to see that Gerry had returned.

"Gerry! Glad to see you made it back all right. We were starting to become concerned," I said.

"I'm glad to be back too. It was kind of a fun trip actually. At least, it was until I started tipping over when I hit rough patches. Then later, as if that hadn't been enough, the machine I was on broke down. The drive belt broke. There was a spare in the machine, but once we got it on, we were never able to get it to work properly. Trying to fix it took a lot of time too. In the end, we just towed it to the side of the highway, doubled-up on the good machine and made it the rest of the way into town.

"The next day, Kevin persuaded someone with a snowcat to take us back for the snowmobile we'd abandoned. You know what a snowcat is? One of those tracked vehicles with a big cab, like you see in movies. Id never seen one up close before. Anyway, we went back in the snowcat, attached a tow cable to the snowmobile, which Kevin rode on to steer, and then towed it back to the garage in town.

"Unfortunately, by the time we got it there, and the mechanic had figured out the problem and got everything fixed it was too late to make the return trip back here, so we had to stay the second night too. This morning we were able to come back though, and here I am."

"What's happening with the roads?"

"The plows and sanders cleared most of the Banff townsite yesterday, and they're out working on the main highway right now. In fact, we passed some of them on the way here. The highway department says they think that they'll have at least one lane of the highway clear by this afternoon and the whole thing by tonight. As long as it doesn't snow again, they think they'll be able to clear the road from the highway to the gondola station by tomorrow afternoon."

"That's encouraging. How about the power and phone lines?"

"We talked to the power company. They said they'll have crews out as soon as the highway is passable, but that the lines are down in several places and they may have lost a transformer station. Their best guess seems to be that we might – just might – have power by tomorrow afternoon. As for the phone lines, the telephone company says they'll have crews out as soon as they can, but that they have no idea where the lines went down or if they went down in more than one place, so they wouldn't even make a guess at when the lines will be restored."

"Well, I'm glad you're back anyway."

"Thank you. There is one small bit of good news. We were able to bring back a way to communicate with the outside world."

"Really?"

"Yes, one of the park wardens was able to loan us a VHF radio. It's one of the ones they install in the park trucks, so it's much more powerful than a handheld unit. They also loaned us a power converter for it, and a big base-station-type antenna we can set up somewhere high above the lodge. They say that it will get a signal to the nearest repeater station, which will then pass the signal along to their radio room in Banff. With the radio, Dianne will be able to talk to the hospital, if she needs advice. The original idea was for Dianne to be able to request a helicopter to get Sandra out, if necessary, but Pat has just told me that she didn't survive her injuries. And Gary gone too? I can't believe it. It's like something out of a horror movie."

"I agree. Did Pat get a chance to tell you about her own close call?"

"Yes, she did," he said, turning to look at her. "See what happens when I leave you alone for a few days?"

"Serves you right for leaving me!" Pat riposted.

Seeing that her natural good humour was retorted, I decided that she was well enough for some questioning.

"You do know how dangerous it is to have a fire burning without the flue-damper open don't you?"

"Of course I do! That's what bothers me the most. I love this room so much that I've spent time sitting in front of the fire before bed every evening that we've been up here and, even though I've always left the damper open during the day, I've checked it anyway every night before lighting the fire."

"And you're sure that you checked it last night?"

"Yes, absolutely. The only thing I can think of is that it slipped closed on its own, or maybe a draft of wind came down the chimney and pushed it closed."

"If so, they must have installed pretty cheap, low-quality fireplaces when they built this place," said Gerry, sounding angry.

I didn't argue with them, but I did make a mental note to track-down George and ask his opinion on the quality of the fireplace mechanisms.

"And you don't remember anything else besides falling asleep in front of the fire?" I asked.

"No I don't. One moment I was dozing in front of the fire, and then the next thing I remember was being yelled at and shaken awake by Renée the housekeeper. When she got me awake, I felt awful at first, but then I smelled that wonderful fresh air coming in the doors and windows she opened. I never knew air could smell so good!"

"OK then. Thank you," I said, and got up to leave.

"Um, I do remember something from Tuesday night though, but I don't suppose it's important," said Pat.

"You never know. What is it?"

"Well, you remember I said that I'd snuck down to the kitchen that night to get a snack before bed?"

"Yes."

"I saw Gary going off to the generator shed."

"Really. When was that?" I asked.

"It was a few minutes after eleven o'clock. I remember the time, because I'd just looked at the clock and decided it was time to go to sleep, but I wanted to get a bedtime snack from the kitchen first. When I left my room, I saw someone way down the hallway, ahead of me."

"Could you tell who it was?"

"It was Gary. He had his bright red jacket on, with the hood pulled up, so it must have been just when he was going to the front to get his boots on his way to the generator shed."

"So, you saw his face?"

"Yes... No, his hood was up so I couldn't see his face. I remember thinking he looked shorter that usual, but decided it was just a trick of the light and the distance down the hallway. It must have been him though. No one else up here has a bright red jacket like that."

"OK. Anything else?"

"No. That's all. It was only yesterday afternoon that I remembered I'd seen him, but I forgot to mention it to you until now."

That seemed to be the extent of Pat's and Gerry's news, and Gerry's attention was mostly on Pat, so I thanked them both and went off in search of Kevin and George.

I found George almost immediately, and he took great offense to any suggestion that there might have been a quality issue or malfunction with the fireplace.

"Come with me," he said in a defiant tone, leading me to one of the many unoccupied suites. There, he showed me what I already knew. The handle for the flue-damper had two locking positions; set at a 90° angle.

"See how the lever has to be pushed into a positive lock to be either fully open or fully closed?" he said.

I nodded. I'd done this before in my own suite but I turned the handle each way just to satisfy him. At each position the lever snapped into some kind of spring clip or notch, with an audible click.

"OK. Now, the damper is designed so that if someone is sloppy and doesn't either open or close it properly, then the weight of the damper plate causes it to fall so that it's 90% open. That just gives three possibilities: fully open, 90% open, or fully closed. These fireplaces are very well made, and I've never heard of one failing. If the damper in Miss Lansing's fireplace was closed then it's because someone made it positively close. Maybe she just forgot to open it before lighting the fire. She wouldn't be the first one, I can tell you."

I'd seen enough, so I thanked George, emphasizing that my questions were all just routine and no reflection on the quality of the resort or of his maintenance.

I did hear him utter a "Harrumph" as I walked away though.

Finding Kevin proved to be a bit more difficult. I thought he might be working on the snowmobiles or something but when I finally found him, it was in the mechanical shop that was part of the gondola station. The same shop in which Kevin had constructed a makeshift door for the generator shed four days earlier.

After talking to Kevin, I went looking for Kate. I found her in a corner of the lodge's lounge, curled up with a book. There was no one else in the room, so I pulled up a chair and said, "Kate, we need to talk." I had some blunt questions for her.

***

"How did you make out?" asked Don when I returned to our rooms.

"Almost the same as yesterday. George, the handyman, is adamant that the natural gas fireplaces were all inspected and in prime working order before they started letting guests stay in the suites." I smiled rather ruefully. "He was so offended by any suggestion that there could have been a fireplace malfunction, that I got a complete lecture and a working demonstration of how unlikely it is to have a malfunction with the flue-damper."

Don chuckled. "OK, so it was deliberately closed while Pat was sleeping. We already figured that out."

"Right. Also, I think Gerry is in the clear. I talked to Kevin about the snowmobile trip and his story matches Gerry's. So, the only way Gerry would have been able to slip back up here without anyone knowing would be if he was colluding with Kevin. It seems to me unlikely that they're co-conspirators."

"Anything else?"

"Well, we have the mystery of the red jacket."

"*The Mystery of the Red Jacket?*" quipped Don. "Sounds like the title of a detective novel."

"Yes, and it's starting to feel like one too. Here's the thing. I have now collected up four late-night sightings of someone – or several someones – going out wearing a red shirt or jacket. Each one of them was attributed to being Gary, but they can't all have been. Let me relate the list and see what you think, OK?"

"OK, fire away," said Don, settling back to listen.

"When I learned about them, they were out of sequence, but I'll give them to you now in chronological order. Number one: on Tuesday night a front desk clerk saw Gary go out the front door just after ten o'clock in the evening. She didn't see his face but recognized his red lumberjack shirt.

"Number two: later the same night, Pat got up to go for a late-night snack. She says that when she went out, she saw Gary way ahead of her down the hallway heading towards the main lobby, heading off to the generator shed. He recognized his bright red jacket, but didn't see his face because the hood was up. That was just after eleven o'clock.

"Number three: later the same night, another front desk clerk saw Gary go out the front door at about 1 am. He didn't see his face either, but recognized his bright red jacket.

"Number four: on Tuesday night the second front desk clerk again saw Gary go out the front door, this time at about 2 am. Once again, he recognized the bright red jacket but didn't see his face because the hood was up (like it had been the previous night). So, there you have it, four different late night Gary sightings on two nights, and all at different times."

"Seems unlikely," said Don. "Unless on the first night, Gary went out in his lumberjack shirt, on his way to the generators, then realized it was too cold and went back for his red jacket."

"Possible, but then why was he found dead wearing only the lumberjack shirt while the red jacket has disappeared."

"Disappeared?"

"Completely. I've looked everywhere."

"OK then, which ones do you think were Gary?"

"Only the first one. I think Gary was spotted wearing his red lumberjack shirt going out to refuel the generators. That was a heavy shirt, and he already knew how hot it would be in the generator shack so I think he left his jacket behind on purpose."

"That would explain sighting number one. How about number two?"

"I think that was the murderer, on their way out to murder Gary and wearing a bright red jacket for camouflage."

"Ok, so who was number three then?"

I smiled. "Turns out that was Kate. When I was trying to figure out whether any of the people spotted going out the front door were just going out for a smoke, Kate denied being a smoker. I didn't believe her because I'd smelled cigarette smoke on her breath when I was so close to her on the day that Sandra died. When I went back to challenge her on it, she relented and admitted that she'd been sneaking out behind the lodge at intervals to smoke. She said that on a couple of the nights, when it was late enough that her friends should have been in bed, asleep, she'd simply gone out the main entrance, which was closer."

"Her friends?"

"Yes, she was addicted to smoking and had tried to hide it from her health-conscious friends."

"Surely her close friends haven't been fooled?"

"That's what I told her. I suggested she come clean with them, that they wouldn't be surprised but would appreciate her trying to be honest with them."

"What's smoking have to do with whether or not Kate is the murderer?"

"Well, it cleared up one of the bright-red-jacket sightings. More importantly, Kate told me that she'd frequently been joined in her behind-the-lodge smoking by some of the lodge staff. I found two women and one man from the hotel staff that confirmed Kate's story."

"So, how about Gary-sighting number four? No, wait a minute. The front-desk clerk couldn't have seen Gary going out that night. Gary died the night before."

"Bingo! So it was someone else wearing a bright red jacket, and maybe with another jacket or big sweater on underneath to bulk it out. That same someone could have pulled on Gary's hiking boots from the front rack, and then tramped through the snow over to Pat and Dianne's suite."

"Did the desk clerk see this someone come back later?"

"No, but he said he wasn't actually at the Front Desk the whole time so he must have missed whomever it was."

"OK then, someone puts on Gary's jacket and boots, walks over to Pat's living room, goes in the sliding door, checks that she's asleep, closes the fireplace flue-damper, bunches up rugs in front of the three other doors, then slips back out the sliding door, closing it behind them. Then they simply walk back to the front door, wait until the desk clerk leaves his post for a moment, then walk in and drop off the boots, and then disappear down one of the hallways."

"That's what I think, yes," I nodded.

"I bet you've gone around and counted the number of bright red jackets?" It was a question.

I nodded again. "Three, Gary's, Kate's, and one of the women staff."

Watching me closely, Don knew there was more. "And?"

"And Kate has her jacket in her room. The same goes for the staff member. Gary's seems to be missing."

"Ah hah, so you're going to go search for the red jacket."

"Yes," I sighed," but unless our killer has made a slip, I don't think we're going to find it. I doubt that they'll try impersonating Gary a third time, so they've probably hidden it somewhere."

"Would Silver be able to find it?"

"Maybe. We'll try, but I'll be surprised."

Unfortunately, I was surprised, and not just about the jacket.

At lunchtime, I was looking around for Gerry and was about to try the dining room when he found me.

"Hi Alex," he said, "can I talk to you for a moment?"

"Of course," I replied, and was surprised when he led me outside.

"Pat's in there, having lunch with Barry and Dianne. I pretended I wasn't hungry so I could look for you... I was hoping we could have a confidential talk." He raised his eyebrows, questioningly.

"Sure, what's on your mind?"

"Maybe it's because I just got back up here and everyone's telling me their stories, whereas you've all been living it, but I've been thinking about the deaths of Sandra and Gary, and last night's near-miss for Pat."

"And you think we're too close to it all? Can't see the forest for the trees, as they say?"

· "That's exactly it. Everyone I've talked to goes on about all the unfortunate accidents, and how unlucky this trip has been. Unlucky! Look, my research involves a lot of probability and statistics, and I'm always looking for patterns in my data and having to think about the probability of any perceived patterns being real."

"Go on," I nodded. I knew where he was headed with this.

"Look, I'm a physicist. I understand electrons very well, but anything to do with people is a mystery to me. OK? But, but it seems to me that three death or near-death accidents, involving the same small group of people, in a span of only three days is unlikely to be a coincidence. In fact, it's so improbable that it's almost impossible."

"So what do you think is going on then?"

"Well, I can accept Sandra's death as a horrible accident, but I just can't believe that either Gary or Pat were stupid enough, or inexperienced enough, to have succumbed to carbon monoxide poisoning. I mean, I know these people. The circumstances are different, but it's even the same poisonous gas in both cases for heaven's sake."

"So, what then?" I prompted again.

"Well, it has to be murder, doesn't it? Or at least one murder and one attempted murder?"

Gerry the physicist; the thinker, I thought to myself. *He comes up here for a few hours, talks to some people, thinks it all out, and comes to a logical conclusion.* I didn't see any point in trying to change his mind and besides, I was going to need his help, so I simply said: "Yes."

"You agree?" He sounded surprised.

"Yes."

"Well then…" My simple acceptance had thrown him off balance. "What are you doing about it?"

"Investigating. Examining the scenes of the incidents; collecting evidence. Asking everyone where they were, what they were doing, and whether they heard or saw anything unusual on the nights in question. That sort of thing."

"And?"

"And I agree with you. These incidents are not coincidences. We have a murder and an attempted murder, and they are connected." I refrained from telling him that I didn't believe Sandra's death was an accident. He didn't need to know that yet.

"What's the connection?"

"I don't think I should tell you any more just yet. But I do have a warning for you and I would like your help with something."

"Sure, anything. What do you want?"

"Can you quietly search Gary's room and see if you can find that bright red coat of his? And if you can't, can you get me a piece of Gary's clothing. Something he's worn a lot lately but hasn't been washed since."

Gerry thought for a moment. "His pyjamas?"

"Perfect. And can you do all that without letting anyone see what you're doing, and without telling anyone anything about what we've just been discussing? I mean not even Pat."

"Not even Pat, but…" as he paused, I could almost see the gears whirring in his brain. "You don't want to alert your suspects, and you're down to just two suspects now, aren't you?"

I nodded yes. "Try not to think about them, and if you run into them, please try to behave the same way toward them that you always have."

"Distant, impersonal, aloof even, you mean?" but he smiled when he said it. "I know that's what everyone says about me behind my back."

"I wouldn't have put it quite like that, but yes, try to just be your normal self. OK?"

"OK, and meanwhile you'll be working down your suspect list?"

"Right," I replied, "and I only have until tomorrow when the gondola starts up again to find the answers I need."

Gerry just nodded and said, "I'll go search our suite and see what I can find for you."

As he turned to go, I let him get two steps before softly calling out to him. "Don't you want to hear the warning?"

He looked at me for a moment then said: "Watch over Pat. Whomever tried to kill her might try again?"

I smiled, grimly. "Thank you, Gerry, that's exactly it."

"Don't worry," he said. "This time I'll stick to her like glue," and he strode off.

There goes a fine mind, I reflected, watching him walk back and go inside the resort.

Laurie Schramm

8 CONFRONTATION

That afternoon, the skies finally cleared and the sun came out. Although there was still a lot of snow on the ground, Don and I were strongly feeling the need to spend some time outdoors so, along with Silver, we went out and tramped around in the snow. This was made easier by the fact that Kevin and one of the other lift attendants had used snowmobiles to create well-packed paths leading up into the meadows area and back.

Beyond Don and I, the sun had brought out the others as well. We spotted Barry and Diane well ahead of us, walking hand-in-hand. At one point, the two of them turned for a moment and glanced back at us. *Is one of them the murderer, or is it both of them together?* I wondered. But I was quite sure that I had my answer already.

Proving it was going to be another matter entirely.

"Those two seem to be getting along well," said Don. "Looks to me like they're going to be a couple again."

"It sure does," said a voice. It was Pat who, with Gerry and Kate, had come up behind us.

"How are you feeling Pat?" I asked.

"Much better, and even better now that we can get outside in the sun and fresh air again! Must be something to do with the carbon monoxide I took in, but all of a sudden I just love the smell of fresh air." She certainly sounded like her old self again, so that was a relief.

"How about you Gerry? Recovered from the rigours of your

105

snowmobile trip?" I asked.

"Oh sure. Not much to recover from," he said with a smile. "It was a lot of fun. Trying to control the sled in the fresh powder was tiring, but it was worth it."

Gerry, I noticed, seemed to be warming up to us, as he'd said more to me, at least, in one day than he had the whole rest of the time since we'd first met on the Friday before. Unless I missed my guess, the week's experiences were bringing Gerry and Pat closer together too, which may have contributed to his becoming a bit more outgoing. Whatever the reason, it was a positive change.

I think Silver must have been the happiest to get out of the lodge for a while. I'd left him off-leash for our walk, and he took full advantage of his freedom by bounding here and there through the deepest snow drifts he could find. Then, he'd race back to us stand there for a moment, panting with his tongue out and giving us his wolfish smile. Then, he'd race off, puppy-like, towards another snow drift and do it all over again. I had to laugh, as watching him made me feel younger and more relaxed for a few moments.

Together with Gerry and Pat, we continued our tramping through the snow and chatted about whatever came into our heads. Everything and nothing, if you know what I mean. At one point we began to compare our favourite places to visit in Canada, which took a while because there were a lot.

There was one point, before we got back to the lodge, where Don and Pat were well ahead of Gerry and I. Gerry immediately took advantage of the opportunity to tell me that he had a small package for me that he would drop off at our room after supper. When I raised an enquiring eyebrow, he chuckled and said it would be Gary's PJs[18]. "They're very soft and absorbent, and he wore the same ones every night, so they should be full of his scent!"

I chuckled, thanked him, and said that I was sure he was right.

That evening, Gerry knocked on the door of our suite and handed me the package.

"No bright red jacket?" I asked.

He shook his head no. "Gone. Not in the room. Not hanging by the front door. Just gone."

I wasn't surprised. I didn't tell him that I'd already snuck in and looked there myself. Instead, I thanked him, said goodnight, and decided that Silver and I would try to find the jacket in the morning. As I was closing the door to our suite, a white ball of fur dashed in. When I'd fully closed the door and turned to look, the ball of fur was settling himself on one of the two comfy chairs in front of our fireplace.

"Hello Merlin," I greeted him. "Decided to come visiting, did you?"

By this time, Silver had padded over to check out the newcomer and for a few moments the two of them simply stared at each other. Being up on the chair, Merlin's eyes were at the same level as Silver's. Neither of them made a sound, and I wondered what kind of silent communication was passing between them. Whatever it was, it must have been amicable, because Silver eventually turned away, stepped a bit to one side, and laid down on the floor in between the chairs and the fireplace. Apparently, hostilities were not in order, so I relaxed and took the other chair so that, when Don came into the room a few minutes later, he was surprised to find all three of us sitting sleepily before the fire.

"I wonder if we could adopt him," mused Don. "There can't be many cats around that can get along with Silver so well."

Day 8: Friday, October 26, 1979

In the morning, while the other guests were either sleeping-in or having breakfast in the dining room, Silver and I went on a hunt for the missing red jacket. Giving him a good sniff of Gary's PJs, I set Silver to tracking. We first tried all of the lodge's hallways and public rooms, except for the dining room, then went outside where Silver carefully searched the entire perimeter. He seemed to catch some traces of the scent where the trampled pathways in the snow led to the ancillary buildings but he didn't find anything in the generator building, nor in either of the general storage sheds for which Marcel had loaned me a key. I even checked underneath Sandra and Gary's bodies, in case our murderer had been getting their ideas from Hollywood murder mysteries, but there was nothing there either.

It was only when we approached the upper gondola station's machine shop that Silver began to check and recheck various spots, an indication that he was having some success. After some circling on and off the tracked pathway, he eventually decided that the scent led inside and promptly sat down beside the door, waiting for me to open it for him.

As we entered the machine shop, there was enough light for us to be able to move around without running into things, but much of the shop was dark and shadowy. I was going to go and search for a light switch when I noticed that Silver was following a scent trail. He would still stop from time to time, sniffing here and there, but he was clearly moving towards a gondola car that had been separated from the main cable and brought into the shop on an overhead rail siding. The car's double doors had been slid open, and Silver hopped in. As I approached, I could see that he had picked up something in his jaws. Something bright red. It was undoubtedly Gary's jacket!

"Good boy Silver!" I was saying, and then stopped when I saw the doors of the gondola side shut. *That's strange*, I was thinking, when I sensed a blur of motion with my peripheral vision. I was just turning my head to see what it was when I felt a sharp pain in the side of my neck. I immediately tried to turn around to see what – and who – it was, but whomever it was had quickly slipped their arms underneath my armpits and then brought their hands up behind my head, placing me in a headlock. I immediately raised my own arms in an attempt to break the headlock, or at least loosen it enough to be able to slip down and out of it, but they had a firm grip. I next tried to bend quickly at the waist, in hopes of throwing my assailant over my head, or at least to one side, but they had moved their feet apart and set their centre of balance well back, so that didn't work either.

Meanwhile my assailant hung on firmly without saying a thing.

As I tried to think of what else to try, I found a kind of blackness coming over me. It was becoming increasingly hard to think and, although my pulse and breathing must have been racing, time seemed to be slowing down.

As I continued to struggle, probably somewhat aimlessly at this point, I remember my eyesight blurring, having a fleeting sensation of losing my balance, and then… nothing.

***

When I regained consciousness, I could hear Silver barking and I found myself standing upright with a gag in my mouth, something around my neck, and my arms raised above my head. Naturally, the first thing I did was to shake my head, as if to clear it. That was a mistake!

When the pounding sensation in my head faded, I cautiously looked up to see what was holding my arms up. My hands were tied together with a thick-looking rope that seemed to be secured to an overhead beam.

"Awake, are you?" said a voice in the dark.

"Hello Dianne," I would have said, were it not for the gag in my mouth.

"From the tone of your attempt to speak, I'm guessing that you're not surprised to see me," she said, stepping out of the shadows.

I gave up trying to speak and just shook my head no.

"That's what I thought. Hang on a moment and maybe I'll explain." She walked over to where two thick ropes came down from somewhere up above and were secured to a wall. Untying one rope, she pulled on it and I immediately felt something tighten around my neck. In fact, it tightened so much that I had to stand perfectly upright in order to be able to breathe. Reattaching it to the wall, she untied the other rope and let it fall to the floor. That allowed my arms to come down, although my hands were still tied.

"In case you're wondering what happened to you, I gave you a shot of propofol. It's a new anesthetic we're working on at the hospital. As you can attest, it's very fast-acting but doesn't last very long. You were only out for about ten minutes."

She turned her head to one side and looked at me in a clinical sort of way for a moment. It was as if she was observing a lab rat or something, I thought, and this was borne out by her next comment.

"I'd like to know what you were feeling as you went under, and again as you came out of it but not badly enough to risk taking that gag out of your mouth." Then, she changed subjects.

"I'm sure you can feel the rope around your neck," she continued. "It's tied in a knot that you won't be able to untie with your hands bound like that, and especially not when it's under tension like it is, but go ahead and try if it'll make you feel better.

"Here's what's going to happen. You may not know it, but you're standing on a wooden box. When I kick the box away, the weight of your own body will tighten the rope enough to asphyxiate you. Then I'll untie your hands and remove the rope that was holding them. That way, maybe they'll think it was suicide.

"I'm afraid that it will be a slow death. Sorry about that, but I didn't have time to come up with anything fancier."

I believed her. The rope felt prickly and tight around my throat, and I had to concentrate to repress the urge to panic. I was sure that she'd already killed twice and attempted a third time, and I believed that she'd kill me with no more hesitation that she would have in stepping on an ant or a spider. I would have liked to have tried reasoning with her, but in her present mood I doubt that she'd have listened. She certainly had a range of attributes beyond her medical training and skills. I'd met a careful-planning, patient Dianne – the one that had been slowly poisoning her sister. I'd met an opportunistic, risk-taking Dianne – the one that had killed Gary and attempted to kill Pat. Now I was seeing a desperate Dianne – the one that was gambling her entire life on an impossibly long-shot attempt to make my death look like suicide and get away with it.

It was all academic anyway. I could feel the effects diminishing from whatever drug she'd used on me but I was still securely gagged and unable to free my hands.

I was jarred out of my thoughts by Dianne's next comments.

"If you're wondering what tipped me off," she continued, "I'll tell you just a little. Pat told me that she'd seen Gary going out to the generator shed on Tuesday night, but of course it wasn't Gary at all, it was me wearing Gary's red coat and it was much later than that when Gary himself had gone out. Since she unfortunately recovered from the little accident that I'd arranged for her, I figured it wouldn't be long before she told you about telling me as well.

"I'm sure you have many more questions for me now, but I'm not in the mood. If we were in the movies, at this point I suppose I'd confess and give you a complete explanation for everything in order to show you how smart I am, but this is real life so... Bye-bye now."

And with that, she started towards me, but stopped at the sound of another familiar voice.

"Would you be willing to tell me your story?" asked Barry, stepping out from another shadow.

"Barry? How long have you been here?"

"Only a few moments. I'd been looking for you and heard the dog barking. I thought he was in trouble, so I came in to see what was the matter. I was looking for him when I heard the bit about Gary. I have to admit that when Don told me about the exhaust pipes coming loose in the generator shed it sounded fishy to me. All these mechanically inclined and inventive people don't go to all the trouble of jury-rigging exhaust pipes and pushing them through a makeshift wall without finding a way to secure them. It means that you arranged for his 'accident' too, didn't you?"

"Barry, listen..." began Dianne, but he kept on talking.

"And I see now why Alex spent so much time investigating everything and questioning everybody. Something made her suspicious of Gary's death, then Pat's 'accident' must have confirmed her suspicions. And, if you add Gary and Pat's 'accidents' together, then you just about have to wonder about Sandra's death too, don't you?"

"Barry no, please stop," said Dianne.

"That's where it all began, wasn't it Dianne? With Sandra, I mean. I know how upset you were when we broke up, and losing me to your sister must have made the blow even harder to take. I'm sorry about that, I always have been, but it's always been Sandra that I loved. We wouldn't have been happy if you and I had stayed together you know."

"No Barry, it's not true. We were made for each other," exclaimed Dianne, but Barry seemed not to even hear her.

Silver, meanwhile, was continuing to bark and howl, and to paw at the closed doors and windows of his gondola-car-prison, but Barry didn't pay any attention to him.

"I always thought that you blamed me," he continued, "and I was willing to pay the price for that. But I see now that you blamed Sandra, didn't you? You probably thought that she somehow stole me away from you, but she wouldn't have – and she didn't... So, what did you do? There she was, starting to come out of her coma. Making more and more progress. And then suddenly she dies. How did that happen? But it would have been so easy for you, wouldn't it? Her doctor, her sister; the person that was constantly at her side?"

"Barry!" Diane put a hand up and over her mouth.

"She couldn't move her body yet, much less her head or arms," continued Barry, in a reflective yet relentless manner. "All you would have had to do was pinch her nose, put a hand over her mouth, and wait. There would have been no struggle; no bruises; no marks… That's what you did wasn't it?" He looked her straight in the eyes for the first time., which seemed to make Dianne wilt.

"And you must have killed Gary too then. Right? Why not just dump him then, unless you wanted to be a… That's it, isn't it? You wanted to play the grieving girlfriend so we'd each have a personal loss; a connection; something to help bring us closer together. That was pretty smart really, and it worked. I wouldn't have been interested in rekindling our old relationship, but companions in grief worked like magic on me. Damn you anyway! You had no right to kill her, much less poor Gary." Barry's anger rose as he talked his way through the logic of it all.

"It was for us, Barry. I did it all for us. We can be together now. Just the two of us. The way it was meant to be." Her voice faded a bit, as she said these last few words. I think it was because she could read the look in his eyes.

I was able to read the look in his eyes because he was standing not far away, and right in front of me. His face wore an expression of wretched, hopeless horror.

There was a mechanical noise then, that I couldn't at first identify. It was the gondola system starting up again. I could just barely turn my head enough to see that the gondola cars were starting to move past the big open doorway that connected the machine shop with the large chamber in which the upper bull-wheel moved the cars around to where they could be loaded for the trip downhill.

I couldn't see her, but I heard her say "I did it all for us Barry. I love you!" and then the sound of her running away somewhere.

Barry just stood for a moment, frozen by the need to decide whether to run after her or to come and help me.

He decided on me.

Running over to the wall, he untied the rope that was holding me up by the neck, then ran over to support me as I crumpled down and off of the wooden crate I'd been standing on. It took him a few moments to remove the noose and then untie the gag and my hands.

112

"Thank you, Barry," I said. "I'm sorry about Dianne."

"You're welcome," he said, shaking his head. "I had no idea she was carrying so much resentment, and... hate. And it was for Sandra, when it should have been directed at me! And then to go after Gary and Pat – it's like a nightmare. It is a nightmare."

He looked at me then. "You knew. Didn't you? You knew what was going on, and that it was her."

"Not at first. It came together in pieces and then, even when I thought I knew what was going on, I still had to figure out the who and the why. Eventually my suspect list came down to just you, Dianne, or Kate. I couldn't figure out any kind of motive for you, so that just left Dianne and Kate and the possibility that one of them wanted you back and was trying to eliminate the competition – Sandra. Everything else just followed from that."

I looked over to where Silver was continuing to bark, almost non-stop in the gondola car that had been separated off onto a rail siding. "By the way, would you mind letting Silver out of that gondola car. He's been worrying about me, and I think I need to just sit here for a few moments."

"Sure," he said and went over to open the car doors. Silver was out in a bound and virtually flew over to me. "It's OK Silver," I said as he plastered me with licks. "I'm OK now."

"If you're OK, I'd better go after Dianne," said Barry.

"I'll come with you," I said, struggling to get up. Barry helped me, and then kept a hand on my arm until he was sure I could safely walk unaided.

There were no staff members in sight at the upper gondola station. I later learned that it was being controlled from the lower station and that, with the power just having been restored, they were just testing the system and had no intention of letting any passengers get on, to go up or down the mountain. There were, however, two pairs of binoculars by the upper control panel so I grabbed one and handed the other to Barry.

"All the cars seem to be empty," said Barry, who was quicker to line up his binoculars. "There's no one... Wait a minute. There! Look at the sixth car out, the red one."

"That's got to be her," I confirmed. "Maybe we can reverse it."

We dashed back into the upper control room and looked around. Most of the controls were a mystery to us, but there was a very conspicuous button with a bright red top that was labelled

'Emergency Stop.' Barry pushed it and we immediately heard a loud bell begin to ring, after which the gondola system quietly stopped.

The next thing we heard was the crackling sound of a male voice coming over an intercom. "What's going on up there?"

Barry found the intercom box and pushed the talk button. "Someone got into one of the cars accidentally," he improvised. "Can you back this thing up?"

"No. This model only goes in one direction. If someone wants to go back, all they have to do is stay in the car and ride it back up the mountain again... Say, who is this anyway?"

At the same time, the gondola system started up again.

"Damn. I'm going to go down there and see if I can catch up to her on the ground," exclaimed Barry, and made as if to jump into the next gondola car.

"Barry, wait," I said. I had moved back outside and was again looking through my binoculars. I'd seen something he hadn't. "I think she's going to jump."

"What? No! Where?" He raised his binoculars to his eyes again and began scanning to find the car carrying Dianne.

"Think Barry! You might not want to see this." But he did of course. It was natural. I would have done the same.

As Barry and I watched in dismay, Dianne stuck both legs out of the gondola car's side window, which I'd just seen her open. Then, her waist came out and she rolled over with her face towards the car, so that she could bend her body and slide the rest of the way.

She hung there for a few moments, with both hands holding onto the top of the lowered window and the rest of her body hanging straight down; swaying a bit with the motion of the car.

"No, no, no," moaned Barry, unable to look away.

Dianne was past the point of no return, and I knew that it was only a matter of moments before her strength gave out. I wondered what was going through her mind at that moment. We'll never know, because a second or two later she either let go or lost her grip.

She'd chosen her moment well, from a certain point of view, in that she fell at the point where the gondola car was separated by the greatest distance from the ground below – a dizzying height.

Laurie Schramm

9 EPILOGUE

Although I didn't think that there was much chance of Dianne surviving her fall, with the right body angle and the large banks of fresh power snow there could be a chance for survival. That would mean a painful assortment of broken bones at the very least.

It didn't take very long to find Kevin and ask that he come with me by snowmobile to check on Dianne. It took much longer to persuade Barry to stay back and watch over Silver for me.

Kevin attached one of the Ski Patrol's rescue sleds to the back of his snowmobile, brought another one out for me, and the two of us headed down the winding road that led down from the upper gondola station. For the first while we simply followed the track that he and Gerry had made when they went down the mountain and back, but we soon had to branch off to one side to make our way to where I had seen Dianne fall. Being the more experienced snowmobiler, Kevin went first and broke trail for me.

As it turned out, we had no trouble finding Dianne, as her dark clothing stood out starkly against the pristine while snow. She was lying in a crumpled heap.

Death had probably been instantaneous.

With Kevin's help, I loaded her body onto the rescue sled and covered it with a space blanket that came with it. Then, we both instinctively looked straight up at the gondola cars passing high up above us.

"Except for the terror of the fall, I don't think she'd have had time to feel any pain after she hit," offered Kevin, searching to find

117

some kind of solace in the horrible scene.

"No," I said, "her face looked so calm. She was a gambler. I think she knowingly risked everything and lost, and she took this way out with some kind of grim resolve. What a waste!"

When we got back up to the lodge, we put Dianne's body alongside those of Sandra and Gary. Then, I used the VHF radio that had been brought up from Parks Canada to call the Chief Warden in Banff and summarize the chain of deaths that we'd experienced, and to request that he pass my information along to the local RCMP Detachment and also the Office of the Chief Medical Examiner. That got a number of wheels turning in Banff, so that a number of people began arriving later that afternoon.

There were people to gather the three bodies, and two investigators from the Banff RCMP Detachment came to interview people about Dianne's death specifically. They had a long talk with me, of course, and I turned over my notes and rolls of film from the investigating and interviews I'd done regarding the two previous deaths.

With both Sandra and Dianne gone, Barry seemed to end up in Kate's care and they left on the gondola as soon as the interviewers were finished with them. No doubt they wanted to get away from the scene of the multiple tragedies as quickly and completely as they could. Don and I wondered whether their old relationship would be rekindled, but we never found out.

I was exhausted after my lengthy session with the investigators, so Don and I decided to stay at the lodge for one last night. So did Pat and Gerry, which was nice because they were good company. So was Merlin, in fact, who joined us in taking another stroll around the lodge. Or, at least, along the cleared walkways from which the sun was rapidly removing the last of the snow.

It was quite something to watch Merlin and Silver walking along so companionably, and it was the first time I'd encountered a cat that was unfazed by the snow or the water from the melting snow. It seems that he came from a hardy breed. Despite, or maybe because of, his playful swipe at Don of a few days earlier, Merlin and Don seemed to be becoming fast friends, and he even mentioned that he wondered whose cat he actually was and whether he might be for sale!

Day 9: Saturday, October 27, 1979

The phone service had been restored overnight. There had been a point at which I had wondered whether the murderer might have manually cut the phone line to prevent anyone calling out. As it turned out, however, there was an innocent explanation. There had been a highway accident during the blizzard, leading to a large transport truck crashing into a telephone pole. This had taken the phone lines down.

With the phones restored, I placed a call to my boss in Ottawa to fill him in on what had happened, and my role in it all, which left him suitably amazed. It didn't temper his sense of humour however, and I wasn't able to get off the line without some good-natured ribbing about my seeming inability to take a vacation without police work encroaching (his words), and the possibility (he added) of me being a virtual magnet for crime and intrigue.

We saved our last goodbye for Merlin who, it turned out, was a much-loved part of Marcel's family. After that, we rode the gondola down the mountain and took our last looks out at the beautiful scenery.

"I'm thinking maybe I should get a cat," said Don.

***

It was some time after, with vacation over and having returned to Ottawa, that I was able to see the lab analysis on Sandra's *crema de belleza* facial cream back. It had contained 40% mercury; more than twice as much as would have originally been present in the product when it was purchased, and thousands of times more than would be considered safe in most countries. Clearly, it had been spiked with additional mercury that Dianne could have easily stolen from the university hospital where she worked.

Sandra's post-mortem showed very high levels of mercury in her body, as I had expected. The mercury levels were more than enough to have caused the symptoms I had observed, and the post-mortem report even speculated that the mercury may have contributed to her coma[19], which was a surprise to me. All that mercury, however, was only listed as a contributing cause of her death. The primary cause of death was assessed as being asphyxiation, despite the absence of bruises, marks, or other signs of a struggle or obstruction.

So, as I came to suspect, Dianne had been slowly and cautiously poisoning her sister. If she had simply stuck to her plan, she might even have got away with it. But, when presented with the opportunity, Dianne had seized the chance and taken more drastic action. Unfortunately, that caused a chain reaction that led to her murdering Gary, then attempting to murder Pat and, eventually, me.

After Dianne had jumped from the gondola car, I had searched the mechanical shop and had found the syringe Dianne had stabbed me with. I'd sent that in for analysis as well, and the lab report said that the residual 'liquid' in the syringe was an emulsion of propofol[20], just like Dianne said. Propofol was being studied in the hospital research lab Dianne had been working in, so that explains where she got it and how she knew about its properties.

As for me, I was glad to have been able to bring Dianne's murdering to a halt. It certainly threw Don's and my vacation plans for a loop, but we did get the change of pace and scenery that we wanted. Setting aside – if that's possible – the murders, the attempted murders, the intrigue, and having been snow-bound, it had been a beautiful spot to spend a week. As I was reflecting on this when we rode the gondola down the mountain to begin the journey home, I was reminded of something my best girlfriend used to say: "A change is as good as a rest."

That, I decided would have to do.

As if the weather gods had somehow read my mind, the skies opened up at that point, the last of the clouds began moving away, and the bright sun brought the air temperature back up above freezing.

I felt grateful to be alive.

***

… Alex and Silver will return,
in *"An Instructive Mountie."*

Laurie Schramm

.

SUMMARY

RCMP Corporal Alex Houston, her fiancé Canadian Forces Captain Don Harrison, and her friend and partner Silver make a late-fall visit to a brand-new ski lodge high up in the Canadian Rockies. After only a short period of hiking and mountaineering in this idyllic setting, their vacation is threatened by a snow-storm that cuts off both power and access to the lodge. While they and a group of university students wait out the storm, a suspicious death puts Alex on the trail of a murderer.

Laurie Schramm

ABOUT THE AUTHOR

Laurie Schramm comes from an RCMP family, grew up while living in the RCMP Barracks (Depot Division) in Regina, Saskatchewan, and spent several summers working as a civilian for the RCMP while in high school and university. Early personal influences included not only the real-life RCMP culture but also Hollywood's versions via such classics as *Rose Marie*, and *Susannah of the Mounties*. Many of the events described in this novel are based on the author's real life, although not necessarily within an RCMP context.

For more information, see Laurier L. Schramm on **Linked** in

and:

www.laurieschramm.ca

or

www.facebook.com/LaurieSchrammBooks

Laurie Schramm

ENDNOTES

1. A fume hood, of the kind found in most chemical laboratories, is waist-high cabinet with a moveable front window made out of safety glass. When working with chemicals in the cabinet ('the hood'), the window is left open just enough for a person's hands and forearms to access the inside. Air is drawn into the hood under and through the partially-closed window, and is exhausted through openings in the rear and top of the cabinet. From there, the air is ducted to an exhaust stack on the roof of the building.

2. See *An Intimate Mountie* (ISBN 978-1-7387599-0-3).

3. Light exercise footwear is frequently referred to in Western Canada as runners; in Central Canada as running shoes; and in Eastern Canada as sneakers.

4. The Maine Shag, or Maine Coon, is one of North America's oldest natural cat breeds, originating in Maine, USA and named for their distinctive, raccoon-like tails. Their bodies tend to be broad chested and muscular, with a long, heavily-furred tail, and they are reputed to be able to stand harsh climates. They seem to have originally been prized as mousers, and may have been used as ship's cats.

5. REM, or rapid-eye-movement, sleep is the kind of deep sleep in which most dreaming occurs.

6. A bunny hill is a section of a ski hill that has only a slight incline, making it suitable for beginning skiers. It is usually

located close to the main ski lodge.

7. A T-bar lift is usually used to pull skiers up slopes having moderate inclines. It has an overhead cable that runs over a series of wheels in a continuous loop. Attached to the cable, at intervals, are vertical (recoiling) cables whose lower ends are connected to horizontal, T-shaped bars. A skier catches a T-bar, places it behind their buttocks, and is pulled up the slope while still standing on their skis.

8. An alpine tree 'line' refers to the altitude above which persistent cold, snow, and lack of water make the mountain uninhabitable for trees. The tree line will be at a different altitude on north-facing versus south-facing slopes, depending on whether the mountain is in the northern or southern hemisphere.

9. A mountaineer's altimeter actually measures barometric pressure and has to be periodically calibrated during a hike or climb, usually by referring to identifiable features on a topographical map. To the extent that the barometric pressure doesn't change, the altimeter's pressure readings can be used to determine one's altitude. When one remains at a fixed altitude, it can be used as a barometer to indicate weather changes.

10. In top-rope-belay climbing, the climber is tied-in to a climbing rope, which runs up the rock face, through a carabiner that is attached to a secure anchoring point, then back down to a belayer, whose job it is to mange slack and tension on the rope, and to brake (and then lower) a climber who falls.

11. An adage, one form of which states that: "*Anything that can go wrong, will go wrong.*" The name 'Murphy's Law' may have originated from mathematician Augustus De Morgan, who in 1866 wrote: "*whatever can happen will happen.*"

12. *Macavity: The Mystery Cat*, is a poem by T. S. Eliot and part of a collection of poems about a tribe of cats called *From Old Possum's Book of Practical Cats*, which was first published in 1939. Macavity is portrayed as a master criminal that has a series of adventures with one common theme: whenever anyone tries to find the culprit, "Macavity's not there!" Eliot's cat poems were later set to music by Andrew Lloyd Weber, and brought to life on the stage in the musical *Cats*, which opened in London in 1981.

13. Cardiopulmonary resuscitation.
14. See *An Indispensable Mountie* (ISBN 978-1-7772424-2-8).
15. Multiple sclerosis, a disease of the brain and spinal cord.
16. The World Health Organization (WHO) has warned that mercury is used in some skin-lightening cosmetic products because of its ability to suppress melanin, thus fading pigmentation, acne scars, and general skin tone. However, exposure to any such mercury-containing products can cause mercury vapour inhalation and mercury absorption through skin contact. For this reason, such products have been banned in many countries, including Canada and the U.S., but they remain available through other countries.
17. Up until early in the 20th century, hatmakers often cured felt using mercurous nitrate, which led them to inhale mercury vapours over periods of years. Many of the hatmakers experienced, and exhibited, the neurological symptoms of mercury poisoning. This led to terms such as "Mad Hatters' Disease', 'Mad as a Hatter', and the Mad Hatter in Lewis Carroll's *'Alice in Wonderland'*.
18. Pyjamas.
19. There are a number of documented cases of people suffering adverse effects – including coma - from the use of skin-lightening facial creams that contain mercury. Mercury concentrations as high as 21% have been found in such creams. See, for example: A. Mudan *et al.*, *Morbidity and Mortality Weekly Report*, Vol. 68, No. 50, December 20, 2019, pp. 1166-1177 and A. Boischio and E. Vaught, "Mercury added in skin-lightening products," *Toxicological Note*, World Health Organization, February 2017.
20. Propofol, an ortho-alkylated phenol was discovered and developed (as ICI 35868) at Imperial Chemical Industries beginning in 1977. At the time of this story, it was still an experimental drug. Propofol eventually replaced sodium thiopental in many situations requiring general anesthesia, because of its shorter onset of action (15-30 seconds), similar duration of action (about 5-10 minutes), and its shorter time

for recovery.

21. See *An Inconspicuous Mountie* (ISBN: 978-1-9994940-2-5).

ADVENTURES OF THE FIRST WOMAN MOUNTIE

www.laurieschramm.ca

www.facebook.com/LaurieSchrammBooks

Laurie Schramm

Laurie Schramm

www.ingramcontent.com/pod-product-compliance
Lightning Source LLC
Chambersburg PA
CBHW021919170626
46807CB00007B/2893